Hurricane
Confessions

BY D. RICHARD

DORRANCE
PUBLISHING CO
EST. 1920
PITTSBURGH, PENNSYLVANIA 15238

Dorrance Publishing Co
585 Alpha Drive
Suite 103
Pittsburgh, PA 15238
Visit our website at *www.dorrancebookstore.com*

ISBN: 978-1-6376-4399-0
eISBN: 978-1-6376-4433-1

Hurricane Confessions

CHAPTER 1

*T*oday was a gorgeous day. The sun was shining as Delaney got Reese and herself omelets for breakfast. It was the start of a new week, and Mondays are grueling with heavy mail volumes, papers, and lots of packages. She figured they both could use an extra dose of energy.

"So, Mom, when do you think I can get a car?"

"Reese, you just got done with Driver's Education; you don't get your full license until you turn 16, unless I decide you can't have it until 18, and right now you haven't even had your 15th birthday yet. Don't be so anxious to grow up; you only get to be young once. You got basketball practice tonight?"

"Yep, until 7:00. I just thought I would ask because you know I want the car. The Escort would be perfect for my first vehicle because it is easy to drive, you keep it in great shape, and I want you to think more about getting a Right-Hand-Drive Jeep for your job. You are too tall to keep sitting in the middle like you do. Ya know, I am thinking of your safety as well."

She had to laugh; he makes all good points, and she just could not be more proud of the young man he was becoming. It seems like just yesterday when he was completely dependent on her for everything. Now he is entering the independent phase of life and facing it head-on. He may look like his father, but he is all her to the core. A witty, sarcastic, kind-hearted smart-ass all rolled into an intelligent adventurer. She only hopes when he hits the interdependent phase of life that he finds a partner who brings out his best and loves him unconditionally.

"I'll think about it. I have to get to work, and do not miss the bus. You know I hate it when you go wake up Papa to have him drive you to school.

1

They aren't spring chickens anymore, and last time you startled him so bad when you woke him, he had the jitters all day. I love you, and have a good day at school. I'll pick you up at 7."

"No need, Jay's mom is picking us up so we can go to his house and finish our science project after practice. I think she is making stir-fry for dinner so please have a pizza on stand-by. Another A, here we come, and I love you too. Remember pizza!"

She grabbed her purse and keys heading toward the car. After getting outside, she looked to the heavens and thought, *You did this to me on purpose. You gave me a boy so I couldn't keep all men at a far distance. I have to observe and study them so I can instill traits and good habits in him to ensure he grows up to be a good man. You got one strange sense of humor.*

It is about a thirty-minute drive from Elroy to Trave taking the back roads. She chose to work there full-time because she did not want to know her friend's business. Trave was just far enough from home that it worked out well. Trave was not much bigger than Elroy and was just as rural. She knows people there, especially after being on the same route for five years, but at the end of the day she goes home and leaves that place there. Most of the people she had met during work are acquaintances rather than friends.

As usual she is one of the first to arrive and starts getting right to work. Shelby was still sorting the packages when the others started to arrive. She loves her job, and the people she works with all get along really well. They pick on her on occasion because she is the only one in the office not married, but she picks back.

"Delaney, you should have met this customer that came in on Saturday. He was tall and talked with an Australian accent. Prettiest blue eyes I ever seen. Oh, he would perfect for you."

Shelby just glowed as she said it. Thank God she can't see Delaney's face as she rolls her eyes at the case. Delaney could hear Russell snickering in his case, which was to the back of hers. Shelby only means well, but somehow she is under the impression that Delaney was lonely or something. She is always telling Delaney about single men and crap. Bless her heart, her poor misguided heart.

"Too bad it wasn't Gerard B. and a Scottish accent. He could just stand there, looking pretty as long as he talked for hours. That would be all I need him to do. I probably wouldn't understand much of what he said, but it would be fun trying."

"Hell no, he better not just be left to look pretty," Sasha chimed in.

"Oh we all know she would eventually try to sneak a peek under that kilt," Denny blurted from the far case.

There it was, the office smart-ass putting the final knife in. Delaney was never so thrilled to be on the last tray and about to pack out.

"It would be my luck and all I get a peek at is bag pipes." The office now roaring with laughter.

She began packing out and rolling to go load the car. That part of the morning is always an adventure. She had to figure out where to place everything in her car so that she would not have to make two trips and was still safe. On Mondays every little nook and cranny was filled from the seats to the trunk. About twenty minutes later, she was hitting the road.

Her first five stops are on a paved road and her last eight are as well. Other than that, the rest of her 427 stops are on dirt roads, and calling some of them dirt roads was a bit of a stretch. Some of the roads she traveled were glorified two-tracks. She has two spots on her route that are not her favorite to be on at all. One is a winding two-track that leads about a mile back into the dark woods, and the other is a 90-degree, right-hand turn into a blind two-track surrounded by acorn trees on each side of it. She is not even sure why those two-tracks bother her since she lives on a two-track herself.

She was finished with the first one-third of her route and into the first dreaded road of her route. It always seems to be on that particular two-track the deer or turkeys always want to play "let's test the brakes" game. This morning was smooth, no animals, clear roads, and thankfully uneventful. Coming out of the two-track, she makes a left down to one of two houses on her route she loves. The McBride house, she calls it that because that is the name on the mailbox. It is a beautiful house of brick and mortar with arched windows. To her, it was like an old friend who greets you with a warm hug when you need it most. She rounds the corner, and to her surprise there is a moving van up at the house. She doesn't recall seeing a sale sign. That house has been empty since before she got assigned this route. She tries to pay close attention to the details of her route to ensure she keeps her customers satisfied. Things that make you think. Driving all day in the car leaves you alone with your thoughts a lot. For Delaney, being in her own head does not do her any favors; quite often she overthinks things as it is.

About halfway through her route, she stopped at the gas station to use the restroom, stretch her legs, and get something cold to drink. It is the only spot on her route with those capabilities, plus a little chatting with the cashiers is a blessing when you drive in the car all day and rarely have contact with other people. She usually has packed snacks from home, favoring the green grapes with pretzels and cheese cubes.

"Just keep driving, just keep driving," she sang to herself which she did often. Funny how that phrase comes out to the same beat as that movie.

The end is in sight; with only half a tray of mail left, home was calling her name. After the last paper was delivered for the day, it was time to head back to the office and put stuff away. After unloading the car and putting the mail in its proper spots, it dawned on her she still had to get a pizza. Shelby was saying something about a new customer, but Delaney didn't pay attention to most of what was said because all she kept thinking about was pizza and how good it sounded. Another Monday had been put to rest. Delaney went as far as asking Shelby the name and address, changing it to an active delivery in her book and then did not put much more thought into it.

She ran and got a pizza and a salad because getting the "secretarial spread" was not on her list of things to do. In the Army, that is what they called someone who had a sit-all-day job and their bottom started taking the shape of the chair. "Chair-born Rangers." She hated that nickname because the Rangers had a tough job and she thought they deserved more respect than that. She loved her time as a soldier and did not like anything that resembled disrespect to any service member.

Another beautiful day to go make the money, she thought. She was going through and marking her packages when she came across one she didn't recognize. "Ari Van Ash," she read aloud. Shelby must have heard her because she came right over to remind her that was her new customer she was speaking of the other day. The one that came in with another gentleman and informed them there would be many packages sent often. Shelby acted all clammed up. She was old school, bless her heart; when two people of the same sex came in and were possibly a couple, she clammed up a bit doing her best not to be so uncomfortable.

"Oh yeah, yeah the McBride place, got it."

Delaney packed her stuff out and hit the streets. She didn't feel uneasy around the two-track this morning because the sun was shining through the trees and bringing with it life and warmth. She could see the deer before they tested her brakes. Everything was going so smoothly, and she had her plan to introduce herself to her new customer and explain some of the services they offer. It was turning out to be a wonderful day.

About 1:00 P.M., Delaney pulled into the McBride place and got out of the car and opened up the back door to retrieve the package.

"You expecting anyone, Ari? Female in a white car maybe," as he glanced out the window hearing someone pull in.

A knock at the door. "Mail Lady," which was her normal calling card.

The door opened, and there stood a gentleman, tall with sandy blonde hair, and a nice smile.

"Ari Van Ash?"

"No," as he pointed to the dark-haired gentleman staring at a computer screen on a desk in the dining room.

She could not help but look around. Obviously still moving in, but the inside of the house was just as charming as the outside. Warm and rich colors along with mahogany furniture made it feel so classically comfortable. While she waited for Ari's attention, his friend Jamison was looking her over. He noticed her long and fit legs, trim shape, and her long hair pulled back exposing those piercing grey eyes. He noted she had good posture and couldn't tell much more since her summer dress was covered by a jean-jacket. He did think her tennis shoes were a bit odd with her outfit choice.

"I'm Delaney, your mail carrier. If you ever have outgoing packages you can leave them in your box or leave me a note, and I will come to the house and pick them up. Here is an envelope you can put in your box if you need stamps. Do you have a safe place you would like your packages left if you aren't home?"

Delaney's jacket pocket started spewing out words after one ring; her phone had answered itself, and it was talking loud and clear for all to hear. Delaney doesn't really get embarrassed, but she was caught off guard for a moment.

Delaney, we need to go to TJ's tonight. These kids and Mike are driving me bat-shit crazy, and I need to get the hell out of this house for a bit. I'm sure you are overdue to beat up some damn men on the pool table anyhow. It's Friday and you do not have to work tomorrow so I know you can go out. You have to take one for the team or I am going to end up in a jacket with no sleeves and lots of buckles—you know the one I am referring.

"Hold on, Mazy, I am with a customer at the moment," she said looking at her pocket like it would stop or at least hoping.

"Your chest is talking," Ari pointed out so elegantly while he stared at her with piercing green eyes which were amplified and mesmerizing due to his dark brown hair.

Do you want a cartoon to watch because you being up my rear is driving Mommy crazy? I need a damn break. One day I am going to run away from home or I am going to sell you heathens to the gypsies I swear, screamed through the speaker of her phone.

Delaney quickly covered her breast with her hand to try to muffle the sound of Mazy's voice. Stupid phone somehow got on speaker mode in her pocket and answered itself while with a customer, that's a first. It was a little embarrassing to say the least. She had not been able to find her earpiece for about a week now.

"I apologize for this unprofessionalism. My phone has had a mind of its own lately, and I can't find my earpiece. Here, I have a package for you that must be signed for, and did you decide where you would like packages left in case you are not home? Still keeping her hand over her breast to muffle the sounds of crying and yelling going on at Mazy's house.

"The porch is fine, and I hope you can help you friend.'

"Again, I apologize for this," pointing to her pocket, "and welcome to Trave. It's small but beautiful; we're glad you're here, and if you let me know your packaging needs I can bring them out and drop them off to you. We have express that is guaranteed and insured; just let me know. Again my name is Delaney, and I will be your mail carrier."

She thanked him for his signature and exited as quickly and gracefully as possible.

Getting outside as quickly as possible. "Holy crap, Mazy. I was just introducing myself to one of my new customers who was kind of hot looking and his nice looking friend whom Shelby thinks might be his partner when, how did he word it, oh yes, my chest started talking. I did all I could do to stay on point. Now they both probably think I *am* bat-shit crazy as hell."

"Sorry, I knew you were at work and never answer. It surprised me when you did so I figured you were taking a break. I am about to combust if I don't get out away from the craziness for a bit."

Jamison and Ari watched from the window as Delaney got in her car, skirt swaying with her rapid movement, looking like she was talking to herself. Hearing the part about both them thinking she was crazy made them smile. They just watched as she centered herself in the car and finished her conversation before pulling away.

"About 5'10", ya think?" Jamison asked.

"Yes, and did you see the young Bette D. eyes? It was like they looked right through me and stared straight at my soul. I don't know what kind of training she had, but we got a couple on our staff that could use it. She never missed a beat of her sales pitch even when her chest started talking and screaming."

"I thought it was kind of funny, and what kind of name is Mazy? And of course you saw nothing but the Bette D. eyes. You thrive on the classics. You are so old school. Were they the window to the soul?"

"I don't know, but I am thinking we should go out and get acclimated to the community. What do you think? We should look up this place called TJ's I just heard about."

Observing how Ari looked like he just got hit by a whirlwind, a whirlwind named Delaney, he figured he would find this place he had never heard of. Entering a few letters in his phone, he flipped it around so Ari could see. "They better have food or I am not coming back to help you unpack."

"TJ's Bar and Grill in Elroy, so I am sure they have food. Where is Elroy?"

"Perfect, and about a half hour from here. I hope you brought some clothes because you might stand out a bit in a suit; even if you lost the jacket you still might stand out around these parts."

Ari loved some of the old classic movies, how in black and white the actors and actresses had to work so much harder to convey their meanings. There were a few actresses that really caught his attention by the way they moved, carried themselves on screen, and the way some could look at the camera and make you feel like they were directly talking to you. Bette had sex appeal and expressive eyes, Rita with her personality; Lauren was another who could look at the camera and right through you at the same time.

Ari decided long ago what kind of man he was, what kind of man his parents helped shape. He was a hard worker who never felt the need to keep up with anyone else. He was not materialistic at all, and after his ex-wife, he found that to be a very unattractive trait in women. He didn't like fake or two-faced people. Although he doesn't always agree with Jamison, especially when it comes to women, he knows Jamison is a good man and a good friend. Ari likes to surround himself with people who can have intelligent conversations and opinions that differ and are not friend-ship ends. He has always liked real people who march to their own drum beat.

Ari and Jamison arrived at TJ's at about 8:10. Both of them were starving after moving furniture and unpacking boxes all afternoon. They walked in and quickly assessed the place. Pool tables were in the front of the bar area while a band was setting up in the back half of the bar where more tables were arranged and a small dance floor was located. They chose a front table near the bar so Ari could get a view of both pool tables. He remembered hearing Mazy say something about playing pool. Hearing the specials, Jamison pounced at the prime rib flashing a huge smile at the waitress while Ari went for the Ribeye steak sandwich. They ate and enjoyed the band playing, watching the people entering. Ari figured the prime rib must have been pretty good by the way Jamison was reacting and speaking gibberish in Italian. Jamison and his family had been to Italy about four times; Ari had been there once with them about a year after his parents died. It was exactly what Ari needed to get him back on track in life. After his parents died, he felt lost, kind of how he is feeling at the moment.

Delaney and Mazy arrived at 9:45. Mazy had a similar build as Delaney but was an ash blonde instead of brunette. Delaney looked all around the bar before walking toward the back half checking things out. Then the women walked toward the bar and ordered drinks and a couple dollars in quarters. Ari dropped his head to not make eye contact and noticed she had swapped her tennis shoes for some wedge sandals. Jamison hadn't really thought about being recognized at all and was looking at the dance floor when Delaney and Mazy passed him. He thought about it after the fact.

"That table looks like they play alright. I'm going to put my quarters there."

When Delaney put her quarters on the table toward the back of the bar, she already knew they played alright and they were not from around here. She did not recognize any of them. There were no quarters up in front of hers so she knew not to wander off too far because her game was next. Her and Mazy stood in the archway between the front half and back half of bar watching the band for a moment and the people on the dance floor.

"Sorry, Ari, I think she might have looked right at me as they passed by."

"Don't worry about it; she has seen us once so I doubt she would know who we are plus it is dark in here."

Delaney's game came up after a few short moments. She walked over and picked a bar stick off the wall and chalked the end. Then she slid her hand down the white chalk cone coating the dip of her thumb. Ari watched as she said something to the one man holding a pool stick from the group. The rest of his group sat at the table and watched as their friend eventually got beat. The quarters started stacking up on the table shortly after. They all watched as she played. Ari noticed when she spoke it was short and brief. She never bent over to take a shot only, bent at the knees and crouched. Mazy had sat at the table opposite the group of men by herself. She and Delaney were conversing quite a bit between Delaney's pool shots.

"So tell me about the hot guys on your route, and by the way I am so, so very sorry about that. You know I live vicariously through you, and I would never put your job at risk."

"You are so going to get a huge kick out of this. Next time you go up to the bar to get a drink look at the table to the left in the middle because I am 99% sure that is my new customer and his friend sitting there. I don't know what they would be doing here because it does not strike me as their kind of place. His friend is a flirt, and I think my customer is the shy one. The blond was in a suit earlier, and by the way he is flirting with the waitress. I would have to guess Shelby was wrong, and they are not a couple." Laughing quietly.

"Shut the front door, you got to be joking." Mazy wanted to look to see who Delaney was talking about so badly, but her drink was not even close to gone. It was getting interesting now, and her game was on. Delaney didn't look like she was going to lose anytime soon, so she decided to go the smoking area and check out the two men on her way.

Jamison had noticed how intently his friend was watching that pool table and the woman that was ruling it with a commanding authority; he managed his observation even while flirting with some of the women from the bar. Jamison had not put much stock in the women since he was not from the area, or planning on moving to the area, and he wasn't the one-night-stand type. He figured he could better spend his time trying to help his friend. It had been so long since Ari had been interested in anyone that he felt the need to take some initiative. He watched as Mazy came up to the bar and ordered another drink before heading outside to what appeared to be a smoking area. He did not see the O-M-G that Mazy had mouthed to Delaney on the way back, but he did see Delaney's reaction to her as she passed.

"Ok, brother, wish me luck."

"Why?" Ari wondered.

"You want the 411 on that one" pointing toward Delaney with his eyes, "then I am going to try to go get it from that one," pointing in the direction Mazy was headed. Jamison started moving toward the smoking area hoping Mazy was calmer than she was earlier and would help him out. He would normally never play cupid the stupid, but this was Ari, his oldest and dearest friend. He was starting to feel like a wingman, a position he was unfamiliar with. He took a deep breath and followed the direction Mazy went. He found her and a small group of folks gathered out in a designated smoking area.

"Excuse me, Mazy, my name is Jamison, and I was hoping you could help me out. My friend is very curious about the woman you came in here with."

Mazy, not surprised he knew her name at all, looked at Jamison with that "sure, here we go again" look. "Yes, I can help you with information, but it will probably not do your friend any good. She is a tough nut to crack. A smart, well-guarded fortress, who doesn't let those walls down often."

Hearing part of the conversation, Devon turned and asked, "Who are we talking about?"

"Delaney"

"Good luck, brother, that chick's pants are harder to get into than Ft. Knox."

"Shut the hell up, Devon, you are too young for her. Besides, she knows you went to school and hang out with my son."

"I don't care; age ain't nothing but a number, and she is a MILF." Jamison snickered under his breath and tried to disguise it with a cough. "I would tap you too, Mazy, if you weren't married." Poking Mazy in the side with his elbow while smiling ear-to-ear. Mazy is fighting back a very nauseous feeling at his comments, and now she has to ask her son what the hell a MILF is.

"Sorry, oh yes, Delaney. After her husband died, she and her son came back home, which was about 7 years ago. She doesn't talk about what she did in the Army with hardly anyone; most don't even know that was where she went after high school. She is guarded around most, highly intelligent, like Jeopardy frickin' smart, a crack-shot with a weapon, and most importantly an empath, so she doesn't touch people and is very selective about who she keeps near herself, employed in a government job she loves, and pretty driven. Oh God, I almost forgot, she intimidates most men so he better have an A game. It does not take her long to figure people out; she reads most of them like a book, and she reads a lot of books."

"Intimidates men?" That statement had Jamison a little worried for his friend.

"Yes, intimidates with her strong mind and intelligence. She smells of confidence and drive," which always cracked her up because Delaney never felt she was confident at all. "If you got commitment issues, she will talk about future plans and white picket fences to chase you off. If you are a control freak, she will make sure you have zero power over her. She calls it weeding out the weak, and she is good at it. She is extremely independent, and there is just nothing she won't attempt to tackle. Like car repairs, she came and put in a new toilet in for me, and just for shits and giggles she decided to jump out of airplanes while she was in the Army. She has been to other countries and cultures in her travels. It's crazy, and it also makes it hard for her to relate to some folks."

It was so well rehearsed she didn't even stop to think about what to say. Obviously not first time she has been asked. Jamison picked up on that right away.

"It sounds like she and Ari have quite a bit in common."

"He better have an A game because she will talk herself out of a damn date before she ever talks herself into one. Like I said, she is guarded and is constantly studying and surveying her surroundings. By the way, she already knows you both are here. She pointed ya'll out to me shortly after we got here. My phone call today was embarrassing to her and shook her confidence a bit during work earning you all a mental note in her journal. She will deny it of course and tell you that was part of her military training to observe people."

Both Mazy and Jamison headed back to their respective parties at different times to not draw attention. Mazy could tell by look on Delaney's face that it was almost time to go; she was getting pissed. Mazy was guessing the twenty-something-year- old playing pool and trying to get her to go home with him was getting on her last nerve. This last game she annihilated him, leaving him with six balls still on the table. There were also no more quarters on the rail of anyone waiting for their pending ass-whooping. She plays really good when she is pissed. It was kind of humorous to watch because she looks and comes off as friendly and sweet, but beware, that halo will go askew on those horns she has when you cross her. She calls it from hero to zero in less than sixty.

Jamison headed back toward his table not really sure how eager he was to tell Ari what he had found out. On his way back, he glanced over to see Delaney smile at her opponent, shoot, and sink a difficult 8 ball shot off the rail. She congratulated him on a good game and shook his hand. Then she walked over to Mazy.

"You been gone for a while, Mazy; everything alright?"

"Couldn't be better, except now I think Devon is a P-I-G."

"Why, he is a sweet kid."

"Um no, he is deranged. Did you know he wants to give you the high hard one?"

Delaney almost sprayed Mazy with the mouthful of drink she had just taken. Both women are laughing hard, and the only word that can be made out of the laughter is gross. Must have been an inside joke that the others surrounding them were not let in on. Delaney was laughing so hard it brought tears to her eyes. Jamison was very worried that Mazy was telling her about his inquiry. A bit of panic began to set in hoping that laughter was not about his best friend. Not knowing these women did not help the feeling whatsoever.

Ari was looking at Jamison with anticipation. He was extremely interested in finding out if he learned anything about her or not. He was doing his best not to get his hopes up and really confused as to why he felt like that anyhow. This whole situation was so out of character for him. Chasing some strange woman to a bar and watching her most of the night was just not him.

"Seems she is widowed with child, very smart, Mission Impossible, and intimidates men to weed out the weak. Not my words of course. Her friend says she gets hit on quite often but does not entertain them. Apparently she is extremely picky. She loves playing pool and keeps herself guarded. Doesn't talk about what she used to do in the Army but apparently is very proficient in weaponry. Her friend is very blunt and says you must have an "A Game." Her buddy who said she was Mission Impossible would like to have sex with her and looks to be about 20. Most importantly, she is guarded and an empath so she doesn't get all touchy feely."

Mazy passed by their table to pay her tab and said in passing they would be leaving soon, Delaney was irritated and has had enough.

Ari had been observing her play and noted she played well. She also moved gracefully around the table, concentrating and thinking out her shots. He figured she probably played chess because it looked as if she was thinking two shots ahead. He also noted how the men around her were watching her as well. Two men tried real hard for her attention, but he noticed she gave short answers and very little conversation. She seemed kind of oblivious to most of it. It was entertaining to watch how things unfolded. He also thought that she was getting annoyed with the last guy to play because her demeanor changed and she showed no mercy during that last game.

"How interesting she is; yeah, we should probably go soon as well."

Ari knows he has research to finish and numbers to crunch for the client on Monday. He and Jamison finish their drinks and head for the door. As Ari looked forward, he made eye contact with Delaney.

"Interested in a game?" *waving her stick in the direction of the table which now held no quarters for awaiting games.*

"No thank you, too distracting," Ari replied.

"Really, well if you change your mind and get past your distractions, Mr. Van Ash, it only requires 4 shiny quarters to show me how it's done," *sounding as snarky and condescending as possible with her head tilted to the side and one eyebrow lifted.*

"If you don't mind, and I'm afraid I will have to take a rain-check," Ari replied never wavering from his professionalism.

Jamison looked at Mazy with the same confused expression she was sporting. When Ari replied back to Delaney, he could see the flash of flames ignite in her eyes. It was then that he realized she called him by name so she was not oblivious to them being there, or possibly even watching her. He all of a sudden got a strange feeling he could not explain. As Ari and Jamison headed for the car, that feeling just intensified, a feeling of intrigue and mystery wrapped in a very intelligent package. He wanted to know more, and by the look in her eyes she was not about to volunteer it to him.

"Okay, I have to say I did not see that coming. She called you by name, my brother. We are risk assessment experts; how did we just get blindsided? And did you see the tilt of the head? It had "game over" stamped all over it. I think she just closed the door on your opening. Do you have your laptop in the car?"

"Yeah, it's in the backseat. Why?"

Reaching in the back seat and retrieving the laptop from its case, Jamison set it on his lap and started to type. "Time to level the playing field a bit. What was the name of this town again? Challenge accepted, Delaney the Mail Lady, game on."

"Elroy."

It seemed like the Wi-Fi was taking forever. Ari was doing his best not to get his hopes up because at this very moment he was not even sure if he wanted his hopes up. There was something about that woman that was just drawing him in like a moth to a flame, and he really wasn't sure he liked it. His thoughts were quickly interrupted by Jamison yelling.

"BINGO! She has a social media page; everybody is online nowadays and does not have the privacy settings on. CliffsNote version of Delaney Delisle. Same stuff I mentioned earlier—has a degree in computer and electronics engineering, only 57 friends, and not on here everyday. Holy shit, proud of her time in the Army and huge respect for all veterans, to be expected. Posts are a limited amount, which I think is a good thing. I hate seeing those people who post every moment of their day. 'Here's what I cooked for dinner'—annoying. Alright, let's see what kind of things she posts. Photos first. First photo is a mud-coated pic with a young man at some kind of event, next. Damn, must be a military photo; she is holding a bazooka or something surrounded by about 10 guys with really short hair and a lot of bling on their collars."

Ari noticed Jamison got really quiet and could see him tilting his head back and forth as in trying to study something. Jamison was reading something aloud but not really aloud so Ari could not understand completely what he was saying.

"Well? You're killing me here. Just spill. I am a grown man and can handle it."

"Good thing you are sitting down already. I am trying to figure out if this picture is of her or not. Same eyes but hair is wet, and it's only a headshot so I can't tell or not. If it is not her then it looks so close to her they could be related. Anyhow, picture is not as important and what it says. It indicates she might be a Domme. Oh my brother, you might have to do a thorough risk assessment before you pursue this woman."

"A Domme, as in whips and chains Domme?"

"Maybe, it looks like there are a few more posts on here that indicate the same. We are trained to read, observe, and analyze. "

Just then the computer started to make a buzz sound, and a big blue box that said "connection lost" flashed on the screen covering Delaney's page. After a few attempts to reconnect—having no luck—Jamison closed the laptop and watched his friend's facial expressions the rest of the way home. He knew Ari's mind was going a hundred miles per hour; he could see it on his face. He also knew that Ari was not the type to just go by someone else's word. If he were a betting man, less than five minutes after arriving home he would be asking Jamison to pull up her page again.

"What is an empath? I know I have heard the word before but can't think of what it means. Mazy said it was really important about her; she insinuated more than she was saying so we need to look that up."

⁓

"Delaney, my love, what the hell was that about?" Mazy asked cautiously.

"I believe Mr. Van Ash was indicating I was winning because I am playing pool in a dress and it is distracting. I really don't like arrogance or ignorance for that matter."

"Are you sure that is what he meant, because his friend was out inquiring about you for that man, so I am not sure the word distracting was about your dress. You are probably just pissed by your last opponent and jumped to that conclusion."

"Well did you discourage him for me like usual?"

"I gave him the highlights, but you know one day, Laney, someone is going to come along and knock your walls down."

Delaney laughed but then thought how arrogant she was being and stilled her laughter. She was no fool and did realize Mazy could be right, but it wasn't today by some twenty-something-year-old here in the bar or by a guy on her route that is distracted.

"One day, maybe. You about ready to go?"

"Sure, let us say goodbye to everyone and you can walk me out to the car, ya damn distraction. It's like sending the designated driver out as a decoy before the drunks leave." *Both of them laughing now.*

Seemed like thirty minutes before they left. Delaney could not wait to get home, take the clip out of her hair, and put on her sweats. Nothing like the comfies to make you feel whole again. The house always seemed so quiet and kind of lonely when Reese wasn't there. She snacked on a few grapes on her way to the bed thinking it was time to put this day to bed as well. "Distracting," what an odd word to use she said thinking aloud as she strolled down the hall.

CHAPTER 2

*A*ri had finally stopped thinking about her long enough to fall asleep. He woke up the next morning and finished the statistics and analyzing the data for his client Monday. He only had one area of concern to discuss with the client, a plastic piece to the product that could be a potential danger. Jamison and he had found a local company that could make it out of metal saving them money in the future between shipping cost and liabilities. Bad news was never Ari's forte; he was a good news kind of guy. With everything wrapping up, Jamison decided it was time to head back to Great Falls, mostly because he was craving a green girl coffee and a livelier pace.

As the afternoon approached and unpacking was winding down, she began to dominate his thoughts. The way she moved and her mannerisms he found to be intriguing. He figured if Jamison could find the social media page, so could he. After about 5 minutes, he had found it. Now he could see the pictures Jamison was talking about on the car ride home. He started looking at each picture and post, analyzing every detail. Only twice did he feel a little stalkerish. He was even more confused after looking at all that than he was before he started. His analysis: all over the place. She might be a Domme, possibly a closet romantic, an adventurer, a hidden assassin, a genuinely honest person, and maybe just a touch scary. He found the pictures most interesting. He made note there were very few of her on there. Most of those were a little obscure, like the one of her and her son both pulling back bows up in a tree stand; her face is partially hidden by camo. The one of her covered in mud also obscured. There are a couple of her and Mazy, just a couple, and you can tell they span some years, and most of them were taken in the dark. There is also one of her building something with a little boy taken at a distance so no detailing. Then he remembered her friend calling her guarded. The only clear and highly visible picture was her profile picture, and it was haunting and tormenting. He enlarged it to get a better look at it. Her eyes weren't just grey, they had a sapphire blue outer ring to them. They also show that hint of mischievous fire that he witnessed first-hand. If the eyes are the window to the soul, he couldn't tell if he was trying to see hers or if her picture was staring right at his. It kind of made him uncomfortable the way her picture made him feel. He quickly reduced it back to its original size and decided it was time for dinner.

Then he remembered the word Mazy used, empath. He grabbed his tablet and looked that word up while eating. He learned they are generally non-aggressive and try to be a peacemaker. They see a problem and try to fix it, good listeners, complex thinkers, and care about peace of mind. They sense other people's emotions. The most interesting thing he read: People and animals are attracted to empaths for their light. They are beacons of light and warmth. People are drawn to them as metal is drawn to a magnet, an unconscious reaction to being in their presence.

As he was wandering through the house getting stuff ready for his meeting tomorrow, he noticed her picture still staring at him on the monitor. He looked at it again, studying each detail, trying to figure out why she had an effect on him the way she did. As a realist, he knows this is all him. She has barely said anything to him. *Oh crap, she called him Mr. Van Ash with fire in her eyes.* He is not real sure how much she noticed at the bar because she was busy playing pool and making his second encounter with her not ideal. She kind of surprised him when she invited him to play pool and then called him out by his name. *Shivers ran down his spine.* He closed out the page and shut the computer down. "No more distractions."

Delaney decided to take a quick break from her route and grab a snack. She was dreading her next stop. Of course a package came for Mr. Van Ash a.k.a Mr. Distracted. She was dreading the fact that she felt as if she would have to bite her tongue. Oh, she wanted to give him a piece of her mind about how her dress had nothing to do with how she plays pool. She decided to give Mazy a call, which always helps her calm down.

"What's wrong? You never call me while you are working." Mazy sounded concerned.

"Nothing is wrong. I am just dreading my next stop. Remember the guy from TJ's the other night, Mr. Distracted? I have to stop there next, argh."

"Stop it, Delaney Delisle. I don't think he was referring to the way you were dressed when he said distracted. Think about it; moving in a new place and coming to TJs, sent his friend to me to inquire about you, unfamiliar territory, and I am thinking he is extremely shy and that is a lot of distractions. He didn't take you up on that pool game, and he was polite about it. You on the other hand got a little shitty, and sarcasm is not one of your better qualities."

"I know. I feel a little bad about that. I think I was more frustrated with playing pool against the horny little boy worse than anything else. You are right, and I probably took it wrong and read more into it than it actually was. Distracting is an odd choice of wording, don't you think?"

"If I knew how a man really thinks I would be rich, living on some tropical island instead of here. Better yet, you and I would go to Italy so I can experience what you did because it sounded like heaven. You just have to knock me out for the flight."

That was just what she needed. She was no longer loaded for bear. Instead, she felt a bit of pity for her friend. Mazy has never left this state, never seen the world like she has. She also has never flown anywhere. Her only life experiences come from here, and her only choices come from here. Mazy deserved better.

Delaney pulled into the McBride house driveway, honked, and then headed to the door. Nobody answered as she knocked. The package said no signature necessary so she scanned it and left it on the porch.

Meeting with the client went extremely well. They were so pleased with the risk assessment and the solution to the plastic gear situation. The owner of the company is a huge fan of keeping it local and was thrilled they found a local fabricator that could make his product better and safer. He got right on the phone with his CEO giving him the fabricator's information and telling him to "make it happen." Ari and Jamison decided to have some lunch to celebrate before Ari headed back to Trave.

"You look tired, my friend," Jamison observed.

"A bit, my mailman—excuse me, mail lady decided to haunt my dreams last night."

Jamison began to chuckle a bit. "Oh yes, Delaney the mail lady. Shit, maybe I should stay home one day to see what my mail person looks like. Honestly, I had never even thought about it until now. Our mail at the office is brought in by the secretary, and I am never home to see my mail person. So, tell me about your dream."

"Well I checked out her page, and I think I accidently burned her profile picture into my brain. The dream was erotic without being sexual. I find her eyes to be haunting. In my dream she was taunting me, and it was turning me on. I wanted her. Then she cracked a whip, and I woke up instantly dazed and aware."

"So you think she is a Domme too."

"I am not really sure what I think. I can only say for sure that I think Delaney Delisle is one complex person who I apparently want to know more about even though she kind of scares me a bit. I don't want to find myself handcuffed to a bed with a rubber ball in my mouth and another somewhere else."

Both men cringed at the visual that left in their minds.

"I am going to do a little more research on the subject, but also proceed with caution." *Both men chuckled.*

Once lunch was over, Ari headed back to Trave. It was about a two-hour drive giving him plenty of time to think on the ride home. He began wondering if a woman like her was out of his league. He concluded he did not have enough information to go on yet. There was something about her that would not let him rest. He found himself thinking of her often, mostly about her eyes. That part bothered him because it just never happened to him that he can recall, not even with his ex-wife.

A couple more times Delaney had stopped at his house to deliver some packages. They had idle conversations, mostly greetings. He asked a couple of questions and got short answers in return. He felt he was making zero headway with getting to know more about her. She seemed distant and well guarded. So well guarded he wasn't sure getting to know her better was even possible.

———∾———

It was a rainy Friday morning. A couple of downpours really had things muddy and puddles scattered all over the place—not a carrier's favorite weather condition to deliver in. Today, Delaney just was not happy. She was cold and wet, coated her floor matts with mud. She also knew she had to stop at "Mr. show some skin is how you win, Mr. I'm a distraction in my dress." She has tried to get that thought out of her head, but it just keeps popping in and aggravating her. Who does he think he is anyhow? Good thing I can put on a happy face, service you with a smile, while in my head it's a whole different story. The more she thinks about it, the more it pisses her off. She wants to believe Mazy when she says she was sure he didn't mean it like that, but damn it's hard to control the thoughts. Not to mention, if he didn't mean it the way she took it than she was just being an asshole.

She pulled up Ari's house, jumped out, and knocked on the door. No answer, so she turned around and bolted off the porch a little more hurried than she should have been. Next thing you know, she was looking at both her feet at her head level. *Holy shit.* She caught herself hard on the ground with her hands, forearm, and her derriere. "Son-of-a-bitch"! Her ass made a slap sound as it hit. That mud was cold and slimy. She slowly started to get herself up out of the mud knowing it was slippery wet, looking around to double check nobody was around. She got the keys out of her pocket and popped open the trunk retrieving a plastic bag. She opened both passenger doors and placed a piece of cardboard on the ground between them.

A song by Juice Newton starts playing.

"Hello," Ari answered whispering.

"Why the hell are you whispering to me?"

"I thought I heard something, and I looked out my bedroom window to see Delaney's car down there and she obviously fell in the mud. She is standing between the doors looking around."

"Are you going to see if she is alright?"

"I would if I was wearing more than my shower towel. Oh dear God!"

"Oh dear God what? You bastard, tell me what you see."

"You better be in your office. I told you she was standing between the doors. She obviously is shielding the view from the sides, not from above ho-wever. At the moment she is wiggling out of her muddy pants."

"What is her ass like?" Jamison could not help himself

"Heart-shaped and appears to be firm and fit. Damn, and you were right about the top half. Once she got the shirt off, she looked around again, and she is top heavy. Damn, that woman hides herself in clothing rather well. She has some very long and lean legs."

"Does her bra match her panties?" Jamison inquired.

"I don't see why it matters but yes, and it looks like she tans in a bikini."

"Oh it matters, trust me on that, you lucky dog."

"Not real sure how lucky I am because now I need another shower at a much cooler temperature than my previous one before running to town to get those files that I need to start that risk assessment. Plus, I feel bad because I don't even know if she is hurt."

"Have you asked her out yet?"

"No, I can't seem to make any headway on that research at all. Well guarded is an understatement. Her answers are short and all business. I haven't seen an opportunity yet to ask her out. Besides, she has given me no indication that she would even be interested in a date with me."

Jamison could hear a slight tinge of disappointment in his best friend's voice. Knowing him for the many, many years he has, he knows he has to try to help Ari out. Most of Ari's past couple of dates have been because the woman asked him out. Ari's shyness keeps him from making the first move, that and the fact he overthinks things. He knows Ari is interested in Dela-ney; he had seen it first-hand that night at the bar. Jamison just needed a minute to think.

What is it with these people and their privacy settings? Jamison went to Mazy's social media page from Delaney's. Seeing her green light on, he sent her a message: *It's Jamison from Tj's, who asked you about your friend Delaney. My friend who was there with me, Ari (a great guy), really wants to ask your friend Delaney out but has no idea where to begin. I am asking for your help, again. He makes small talk with her when she stops at his place with mail, but he just can't seem to build the courage to ask her.*

About thirty minutes passed before his computer dinged with a message from Mazy: *If he asks her straight up, she will animatedly decline. She thinks he meant to insult her by using the word distracting. She took it as insinuating she only wins because she was flashing some skin. I didn't think that was what he meant at all but she is pretty hard-headed. Is he shy or something?*

Jamison started typing back right away: *Very shy, a little inverted. He meant he finds her distracting. He is a good man with a heart of gold. Not very good at talking to woman and he is a little bit old-fashioned.*

This time his computer dinged right away: *He is shy and she is anything but. Why would he want to ask her out? She annihilates men.*

He replied: *He is smitten by her. He watched her at the bar, he thinks about her often, and he is quite taken by her. I have never seen him behave like this in my life. She cast some kind of spell on him.*

Mazy returned a message after a few minutes: *She is not a witch, you're funny. OK, let me think about it. If he asks her out she will say no. If she thinks for a moment it is a set-up, I can't even begin to imagine how pissed off she will be. I don't usually do shit like this, especially with her because of how highly tuned in her damn senses are, so I make no promises at this point. By the way, she won't flirt at work. She takes her word and her work ethics extremely seriously. The woman has never even called off sick or ever played hooky. She also takes her promises very seriously— rarely ever breaking one. She's a frickin workaholic and a damn good friend whose friendship I will not ruin over some man wanting to take her on a date, but let me think of a way for him to get his foot in the door.*

Jamison replied back: *Sorry to ask but you are the only one who can help in this particular matter. That man is my best friend and I would walk through fire for him. He needs my help and I need yours.* Then it dawned on Jamison, that one statement in her message stood out and he found it to be odd. He had to stop and picture himself in the bar to remember the word she used. That must be what Mazy means by senses. Empath, it just popped right into his brain. He typed that word in and hit search.

"Oh, shit." He read and re-read what an empath was. Now more of how Mazy had described her made sense. He now understands Ari's uncontrollable attraction to her. Ari has been in the dark so long and she is a light source, but is she the right light source for him? He now clearly understood Mazy's reluctance to trying to help set her friend up. If Delaney sensed it, it could put a riff in their friendship. He would never want something like that to happen between him and Ari so he would never wish that upon Mazy and Delaney. He would be disappointed if she could not help him, but he would also understand. He thought for a moment how hard it would be to be friends with an empath; then he thought about how hard it would be to be the empath. Feeling other people's emotions all the time would suck; sensing your friends lying to you would be awful.

—◆—

Ring ring. "Hello."

"Oh, you are so going to love this. I better just tell you so that you can get the 'I told you so' out of the way. I could not wait until this evening to tell you so I figured I would take a break and call you. So today I have a package for Mr. Van Ash, and I am dreading taking it up to the house because it has to be signed for. Absolutely dreading it! While driving, I am thinking of his word 'distracting' and getting more pissed by the minute. I start coming up with crap like 'flash some skin to ensure you win,' dumb shit like that. Well you can imagine what frame of mind I am in when I get there; then he usually opens the door and makes small talk that seems to calm me and I am out of there. No harm, no foul, right? Today, he doesn't answer the door because nobody is home. So I pretty much run off the porch until I was looking at both my feet in mid-air. Karma, being the ruthless bitch she is, punished me for thinking such rude thoughts about Mr. Van Ash. She planted me straight on my ass in his muddy yard to remind me to stop being an ass."

"Oh my God, are you ok?" *As she begins laughing.*

"I was mud-coated and left my ass print in his yard, but I think the only thing I really hurt was my pride. Thank God nobody was home, because I changed my clothes right there in his damn driveway. I was not about to drive the rest of the day looking like a mud pie. Karma was damn sure letting me know I was wrong and you were right. Show your ass and you'll end up on it.

It could have happened in any other driveway today but N-O, it was his damn driveway. That was karma speaking volumes directly to me. I heard her loud and clear, no more thinking Mr. Van Ash was anything but a nice guy who didn't mean anything bad using the word distracting."

"Holy shit, that is funny. He is going to come home to your ass print in the mud. I did tell you so. I can say that now that I know you are alright. I didn't think he meant anything ill by his statement. Distracting, distracting, distracting. It is just a word, Delaney, maybe the wrong word to use but still just a word. You were already agitated when he said it. Karma kicked your ass."

"No she technically planted me on my ass, which I think may be sporting a lovely shade of black and blue," *as she rubbed the side of it.*

Mazy laughing even harder now, "Well I guess you better be nice to that man and only think good thoughts about him so karma doesn't get you again."

"Yeah, I guess you are right, again. I better let you go so I can get back to work. I am already a little off schedule since my incident earlier. Talk to ya later."

Delaney finished her route with no further incidents and headed back to the office to unload. She barged through the back door carrying trays stacked just high enough she had to turn her head sideways to see where she was going. She did not see Mr. Van Ash standing at the counter, talking to Shelby.

"Oh there she is. Delaney, did you bring back a package today?"

"Yes, Shelby, give me a just a second."

Delaney dug through the trays until she found the one with the only package she couldn't deliver today. She grabbed it and headed toward Shelby. It was then she noticed Mr. Van Ash was standing at the counter waiting, smiling. For a brief moment she began to blush because Mazy's words were playing in her head about leaving her ass print at his place. *Yep, Delaney girl, you leave a lasting impression, an ass print impression.*

Shelby realized the package was coated in mud, and after looking at Delaney she also realized that was not the outfit she left out in this morning. Shelby was anything but un-observant, and she came up with 4 real quick after adding 2 and 2.

"You alright?"

"Yep, didn't hurt anything other than my pride," *rubbing the side of her butt and flinching a bit.*

25

"I can rinse that package off for you before you sign for it if you would like; it would be no problem, and I sincerely apologize about the mud coating it. I lost my footing for a moment this morning. Also if anything in it is broken please let me know and I will replace it."

"It's a memory stick so I am sure it is fine. That won't be necessary," Ari assured them both. "Glad you are alright, although I would put some ointment on that arm"

Just then, Delaney looked at her arm not even realizing she had scraped it. The only thing that was feeling the impact of her fall this morning was her butt. With a hmmm, she went back to her case and finished unpacking the mail. Then she headed home for her other full-time job, her domestic diva job. Honestly, it was her favorite job. She never thought she would experience motherhood, but now that she has, she would not trade it for all the money in the world. Best job ever!

Since after the rain, the humidity was unbearable with the sun coming out, Reese and Delaney decided it was a grilled cheese and tomato soup kind of night. Reese had a game tomorrow, and his coach was on him about concentrating on his footing a bit more. Once the sun went down, they went out to the hoop and practiced a bit until the mosquitoes started to chase them back inside. God, she really did love her life and that kid.

—⁂—

Ding. Mazy's message read: *Please don't make me regret this. Now is the time to strike because she is afraid karma will kick her ass again where he is concerned and no I will not explain that in further detail. He said something about a rain-check at the bar on a pool game. That is his way in. We have to find something that she will need to help him with to hold her attention so she can't just drop off the mail and bolt. Then your guy is going to have to grab his balls and hand her 4 quarters calling in his pool game rain-check. She is a woman of her word so she will feel obligated to honor it and that will frost her cupcake. She will fear karma getting her more than her dreading playing pool with him. After that step, he is on his own. By the way, if he hurts her I will personally hunt you both down—just saying.*

Jamison read the message about three times because he just could not understand the karma part. Mazy could not have been more blunt about the rest though. He had to think of a way that she could help Ari without making him seem unmanly. Good Lord, this was harder than he thought. He gave Ari a call telling him he would be up there tonight after work. Ari seemed a bit surprised. Jamison confirmed it was nothing major but he would discuss it with him when he got there.

Jamison got to the house at about 6:30 P.M. Luckily, during summer it stays light out until about 10. Deer were crossing the roads everywhere, even on the highway. Jamison had to break a few times on the way there making him glad he lived in the metro area. Country living was definitely not his style.

"You still got the pool table in the basement covered in boxes?" Jamison asked.

"Yes, still pretty loaded down, but I am sure you did not just drive all the way from Great Falls to play a game of pool. What is going on?"

"Nope, are you positive you want to get to know the mail lady better? Like 100% positive, not a doubt in your mind? Before you answer, did you look up what an empath was?"

"I'd like to, yes, no doubts. Also, I do not think the empath thing has anything to do with why I find her interesting, drawn to her maybe, but not why I find her interesting."

"Alright then, we need to get cleaning off that pool table and making the basement look presentable. It might not hurt us to brush up on your playing skills since she seemed pretty good at it. That pool table is your way in, and you, my friend, are holding a trump card in the form of a rain-check. She can't refuse because she is a woman of her word and something about karma will get her. Now we just have to find you an opening to deliver the punch line. I am still racking my brain for that one. We also need to have a game plan set; once she is here, you will be on your own. I have no idea how to handle an empath. That takes a woman's intuition to a level way outside of my capabilities. I am thinking honesty is the best policy. Just don't tell her you saw her half-naked; don't even think about it. If she senses this was some kind of set-up, her friend says she will be furious. I think keeping your thoughts non-incriminating is going to be the hardest thing you have ever done. No pressure or anything, but if we hurt her, Mazy ensures she will hunt us down. I don't know her well enough to question it."

They worked into the late evening cleaning up that basement. The pool table cover was finally exposed, and both men carried it outside to rid it of the half inch of dust it had accumulated. No chalk could be found so Jamison said he would stop at the billiard store in Great Falls and ship it to him. Ari remembered she liked to chalk her hand. The sticks were still in the holder on the wall and in good shape. They talked through every possible scenario they could think of, even the possibility that she would feel more comfortable playing in a bar. However, they still had not come up with an opening that would hold her attention long enough to give her the quarters. That part had them both a little stressed.

Time was ticking on by, and neither of them had thought of anything that didn't seem hokey or just not believable. Mazy said it needed to be Friday night, and today was already early Thursday morning. Frustration was setting in. Ari could see his opportunity slipping through his fingers, and there was nothing he could really do about it.

Trees skipping by fast then in slow motion. Crack! Delaney awoke from the nightmare, not real sure if it was the nightmare that woke her or the thunder and lightning. The sky was rumbling with a fury in the wee morning hours. Thank goodness it stopped before Delaney left for work. She was definitely feeling tired. This is the fourth time she has had this nightmare that makes no sense, but she knows it is a foreshadow of things to come. It means something. She hates the dreams that are next to impossible to decipher until they happen. That started when she was young. She woke her mother up once and tried to explain a nightmare about turning on the TV to a channel you don't get and there was a blob and a bunch of other blobs were trying to get it to come back, but it wouldn't come back; it just kept drifting farther away. She was crying and frustrated trying to explain why she was so sad when the phone rang. It was her grandmother explaining to her mother how Uncle Logan had a massive coronary in his sleep and the EMTs had pronounced him dead at the scene. The minute her mother said "Logan," Delaney started screaming. That is who the blobs were calling to, and he wouldn't come back. Then both of them were crying.

Delaney keeps that empath thing a secret. She has told very few people about her gift and her curse, with good reason. A past boyfriend swore she was a witch. Dreams have shown others to be cheaters and liars. Her grandmother even made her swear not to tell her anything else she saw in a dream about her. Her best male friend said he felt her in the car with him during a near accident; Delaney was dreaming about it at the time, and when she woke suddenly, he said the car jumped and only nicked the tree where it would have been head-on. She was wandering through her house, in the middle of the night, when he pulled in and was freaking out on her. She was already having a freak-out moment herself. A day later he swore she was his guardian angel and asked her to marry him. She was 16 at the time; he was 20. Sometimes she views it as a gift when it can be used to help, but most of the time it is a curse and hard to understand, so she keeps it hidden from people, well hidden.

Delaney was cruising right along. She was pulling into Ari's place to deliver a package. *Knocking.* She heard him say come in. He was on the phone and gave her the wait a moment finger.

"Jamison, I am telling you, I already rebooted the computer and I still have a yellow triangle and no internet. I am about to call our IT department to get this going, or I am going to push it off this desk and watch it shatter."

"May I?" Delaney asked.

"Hold on, Jamison."

Delaney walked over to the computer and looked at the screen. Then she looked at the router and unplugged the yellow batch cable from the back of it and from the back of the computer. Then she powered down the router and counted thirty seconds before plugging the cable back in and turning the router back on. After about one minute the yellow triangle was gone.

"Let me call you back, Jamison."

"Go ahead and check to see if you have internet access. If not, you might have to reboot the computer once more. It happens quite often during storms here. Welcome to the sticks," She said with a warm smile.

"Wait, I have something for you."

He stepped into the kitchen and slid four quarters off the counter, walked back to her, and placed them in her hand. She had a very confused and bewildered look on her face before informing him that she can't accept gifts. This made him chuckle a bit out loud.

"I believe four shiny quarters was the price you quoted to collect on my rain-checked pool game. Meet me here at 6 P.M. tomorrow. Does that work for you?"

Delaney was stunned, speechless for the most part. She handed over the handheld so he could sign for the package she was originally there for while she thought about how to answer. Plus she was rewinding the rain-check in her mind like a movie. Holy crap, he did take a rain-check. Damn, damn, damn. There it was; he said it plain as day.

"If we can make it 6:30 that would work better for me." The words slipped out of her mouth before she could stop them or find some lame excuse to not to. *Oh God, why do you do this to me?*

"Deal, tomorrow night 6:30, see you then."

Delaney left and could not wait to get down the road a bit. She could not breathe. Plus she needed to call Mazy. What the hell did she just agree to? She started to curse that filter between her mouth and her brain; she swears most days it doesn't exist, and the other days it's just damn broken. Oh my God, it's not a date; it's just a frickin' rain-checked pool game. How did she not catch that he rain-checked at the moment he did it? She would have countered it then. How the hell did that slip by her? Son-of-a-bitch, I am getting soft.

Ring ring. "Ok, Delaney, whose yard did you leave an ass print in now?"

"Oh shut up, I am so screwed. How did I not catch that? I'm cursed I swear."

"Clue me in here, 'cause I have no idea what the hell you are talking about."

"Ari Van Ash! I just accepted a rain-check he called that night at the bar to play pool. How in the hell did I not notice he said it? But when I started re-calling his exit, I distinctly remember him saying it. I am the queen of the side-step; how the hell did I miss that? You know I would have countered that shit right then and there." Delaney was almost ranting, so beside herself she just couldn't seem to get her bearings.

Silence on the other end of the phone, smiling doing her best not to laugh Mazy had all she could do to reel herself back in knowing Delaney can sense the unspoken.

"Well?"

"Damn, woman, give me a second. I am trying to process it. When are you supposed to play pool with him?"

"Tomorrow evening. Son-of-a-bitch, I am so screwed."

"Chill out, chick-a-dee, it's a pool game. He didn't call it a date, did he? What are you going to wear?"

"No, he did not call it a date, and I can tell you what I am *not* going to where."

"Delaney, don't start that crap again because karma already put you on your ass once for it. Seriously, what are you going to wear?"

"I don't know. I am most comfortable in my sweats. Hey, that's an idea; then I know I won't hear that distracting word."

"Delaney Marie Delisle, I swear to God, you put those sweats on to go play pool with that man and I will personally drive over to your house and kick your ever-loving ass. Just put on a pair of jeans and a nice shirt. It's just a pool game for God's sake, that's all. Oh, and what about those new cute-ass black heeled boots you bought last shopping trip? They would pair well with jeans."

"Alright, jeans it is, and I will call you again tonight after work. I better get back to what they pay me to do."

Delaney got back to her route. Luckily for her, the Johnsons were out primping the flower beds. She liked them because they were always so kind. Mrs. Johnson leaves her fattening chocolate goodies in the mailbox often. Today, it was a cup of ice cold lemonade and some kind words. She also mentioned knowing a nice young man who returned home to the McBride place close to theirs. She reminisced how she knew his parents and what great people they were. How it was terrible what had happened to them. From the conversation, Delaney could decipher that they had died in some tragic way, but she did not have time to ask any further questions; she had a job to get back to, and she was already running behind. She thanked Mrs. Johnson for the refreshing drink and went back to her deliveries.

The rest of the ride was uneventful, which gave her time to think about what had happened today. She was still baffled about her missing that raincheck. It was throwing her for a loop. It happens; it isn't even the first time something has slipped past her, and it seems to happen most when she is already distracted—there is that word again. *Laughing to self.* According to Mazy, she misses men hitting on her all the time. Mazy usually gives her a play-by-play of what she missed later and with great pleasure. Mazy always finds it funny how such a brilliant mind can totally tune out come-ons.

Ring, ring "Was that Delaney?"

"Yes, she delivered me the pool and hand chalk, fixed my internet issues, and took my 4 quarters."

"I'll be damned; you pulled it off. You know I can't really help you from here on out. Message from Mazy says: *Game on but don't be too disappointed if she shows up in sweats. She is very hard-headed and doesn't want her outfit to be a distraction*." *Laughing*. "She has a thing with that word don't she?"

Both men chuckled. Jamison joked to Ari about playing nice to the woman who will probably never wear a dress in his presence again. He wished his friend the best of luck with the most sincerity. Then Ari started talking about how fate had given him the opening by making his internet not work and she had the ability to fix it. Jamison wondered how it happened because his best buddy hung up so he couldn't hear how it all went down. He was kind of thankful because he was not really sure if Ari's shyness was going to allow him to pull it off.

"You'll have to keep me informed of how this turns out. I have to admit I'm kind of curious."

"You know I will. You are pretty much the only person I ever talk to." *Snickering as he hung up.*

CHAPTER 3

Delaney got off work early enough to give her about an hour and a half to get ready. She debated on wearing several different outfits because she was having trouble choosing. She didn't like how her hair was behaving and was all around just unnerved. She began looking for reasons to call this off. Then Mazy called her like she knew exactly what Delaney was up to. Mazy wasn't about to let her talk herself out of this one or find some lame excuse to call it off. Together they decided on a black T-shirt, her light blue jeans, and her new black boots. Mazy told her to relax and have some fun before hanging up. After all that primping and aggravation with her hair, she chose the simple but classic bun leaving a lock of hair on each side of her face which becomes a ringlet just add moisture. A little bit of eye make-up to cover up the fact she didn't sleep well the past couple of nights. She even dabbed a dot of her favorite perfume behind each ear. She topped off her assemble with a black zip up hoodie in case it was cooler this evening. She grabbed her purse and keys, checked herself out in the mirror thinking, *not my best but will do*, and headed out the door.

On her thirty-minute drive to Trave, she second-guessed everything: her outfit, her make-up, hairstyle, her having agreed to this pool challenge, all of it. It seemed like her nerves were getting the best of her and she couldn't understand why. Then her phone rang, and Mazy's voice began ringing in her head, making sure she was in the car driving to Ari's. It was a good thing she called because it seemed to help calm her nerves. They talked up until she was about to pull into his driveway.

Deep breath, get out of the car, you can do this. It's not a date, just a pool game.

Knocking on the door. She felt the overwhelming need to run, but her legs wouldn't move. Ari opened the door and greeted her before she would have made it to the car anyhow. His eyes locked in on hers, and he could not help but smile as he waved her in. He really had a warm smile that could melt ice. He was pleasantly surprised by her outfit. He honestly might have had to giggle a bit had she shown up in sweats like Mazy warned, but the woman could rock a pair of jeans. They definitely showed how long her legs were.

"Hello, I am glad you made it. I was not sure if you were going to, but I am glad you decided to accept my rain-check. The pool table is in the basement unless you would feel more comfortable going out to play. Would you like something to drink?"

"No thanks, at the moment I am alright," holding up her pop. "I prefer to stay here and play if that is ok with you. I had enough of the bar scene lately to last me for a while."

"Definitely fine with me, we can head down to the basement whenever you are ready."

"Lead the way, kind sir."

"This way, madam."

She followed him, watching his every move and listening to him talk. Sincerity and a hint of apology is all she is sensing. Navigating the narrow stairs in her heels was not the easiest thing to do. Then it happened; she missed a stair and fell straight into Ari, almost taking both of the out.

"Sorry, that stair moved," *saying with a smile while looking down at the stairs, kind of laughing at herself.* "Some days I am just an accident waiting to happen."

"Here it is, the 8' Trinity Pool Table."

It is a beautiful billiard table, English Tudor finish, Ram's head legs, and leather woven pockets. The smell of it is intoxicating to her, and the smoothness of the rails made her wish she had one. Mazy was probably right about the fact that if she had one, she probably would never go out to the bar with her again. Mazy goes out to get escape her life for a moment where Delaney goes to the bar to shoot pool and keep her friend company.

"I'll rack them since it is your house and your rules. I usually play straight 8, call all pockets, but not my rules or house."

"Straight 8 works for me."

Ari notices the spark that seems to glimmer in her eyes as she studies the table. Ari is known to be a people watcher. He knows Jamison describes him as shy, but he really isn't. He is reserved. After he observes people, he notices things about them and then chooses whether or not he wants to engage. He was reminded that she was a people watcher as well, however, not sure if she does it for the same reasons. He watched as she racked the pool balls tightly in the triangle. Not a single ball rolled as she lined it up on the dot. He also noted her hands, clean with manicured nails painted in a French tip style. Her nails were simple and feminine, yet kind of ironic their cleanliness due to her occupation.

Delaney has never seen him play pool so she really has no idea what to expect. She figured letting him go first would help with that. She walked over to the wall and lifted every single stick in the case until she found one with the weight consistency she preferred. Then she slid the seam of her thumb and pointer finger down the cone of white chalk. Grabbed the cube and chalked the tip of the stick. Feeling ready for whatever was coming, she turned her attention back to the table. Ari had not broken yet because he was busy watching her.

It suddenly crossed his mind that this could be a one game evening. She was not obligated to anything other than his one rain-check. This was a situation that neither he nor Jamison had thought about. He realized then that that was not going to help him get to know her better. He has to keep her engaged; a guarded and intelligent woman like her needs her brain stimulated to feel comfortable enough to reveal a glimpse of herself. He has her here; now it is up to him to figure out how to get her to want to be here. At the moment he is just thankful she didn't back out.

Delaney unzipped her hoodie, laying it to rest on the back of a leather chair by the pool table. No plans of going anywhere just yet she thought. Time to play.

"Are you a betting man, Ari?"

"For money, no, why?"

"Good, let's make this interesting. If you win, you get to ask me whatever three questions you want. If I win, I get to ask you three. Are you game?'

Was she reading his mind? He was shocked and relieved at the notion all at the same time. This was a solution to the problem of getting to know her better, and it was at her suggestion.

"Any three questions we want and the other answers honestly. I'm game."

He blasted the balls with a thunderous clack, with three of them dropping from the break. He has a run on the 3 ball then the 5 ball. Leaving him with the 2 ball and the 8 ball. He attempted to bank the 2 ball and barely missed. She follows him by dropping the 12 ball in the side pocket, 15 ball in the corner pocket, walks the 11 down the rail, leaving her with the 9 and 13 balls before the 8 since the 10 dropped during the break. She studied the 9 and 13 deciding which one would be the better shot to take. She barely nicked the side of the 13 cutting it sharply into the side pocket. She was lined up to have an easy shot on the 9 in the same side pocket. Barely tapping it, it rolled toward the side and touched the corner of the pocket leaving it to rest in front of the pocket.

"I think you are testing me. I've seen you play, and you would never miss an easy shot like that."

"No, just still adjusting to playing on a billiard table instead of a bar table," she replied.

Ari lined up and shot the 2 ball cleanly into the corner pocket lining him up for an easy shot on the 8 ball. He barely tapped it and watched as it rolled straight into the side pocket. Feeling absolutely elated and thankful that he had practiced quite a bit in the last two days, he began to strategically plan his next move. In his mind, he was debating whether to just come out of the gate charging or gently leading up to it.

Delaney walked over to her pop to get a drink. Thinking to herself how Ari had some skills and she was actually going to have to work at this and focus. Which was already difficult because she thought he was good looking the first day she met him, but then thought how ugly he had become when she thought he insulted her skills; now she was just confused. She was noticing his chiseled details making him more handsome than she originally thought. Plus his kindness and playfulness were hugely attractive to her.

"Good game by the way. I'll rack this time. First question, it's a tough one. Are you a domme?"

Delaney almost choked on her pop. Damn, that was so not any question she would have ever expected. Color her surprised.

"Ok, odd first question to ask, and I have to answer honestly. One second to think how to answer it properly." *After a brief pause to gather her thoughts*, "I do favor my domme tendencies sometimes; however, I wouldn't label myself with any specific category because I like sections of them all. I like to think of myself as creative."

"Explain please."

"Alright, assuming you mean sexually. I like to restrain them sometimes or blindfold them playing as a domme in the dominance and submission; however, I do not get into the sadomasochism or humiliation parts of the BDSM category for lack of better definition. Sometimes, I enjoy being the submissive, and on occasion I like a good spanking and mild hair gripping. When I intentionally dress sexy or do a strip tease for my lover that is my inner exhibitionism taking a lead role; if he likes what he sees or if anybody watches a porn movie that technically defines voyeurism, touch yourself and it is technically narcissism. So I am bit of each without being truly any of them. For me personally, sex should never be about pain or humiliation, but there is a fine line between pleasure and a pleasurable pain that can be blurred. Nibble too hard and for some it's a turn on, for others a deal breaker. I guess I would call myself uninhibited and experimental. For me, it is all about methods of perception using the 5 senses: taste, sight, touch, smell and sound."

Ari swallowed so hard he thinks people in China heard it. Delaney lined up the cue, raised the one eyebrow, and flashed a sinister grin. Game on!

"So no hidden arsenal of whips and chains, check."

"Oh, I'm sure I could accommodate if desired." *Laughing out loud.*

Delaney fired that cue ball into the 9 and all the balls scattered amongst the table. Two balls dropped from the break, and the others were spread out on both ends of the table. She studied the table for a moment and shot the 3 ball in, then the 5 went in. Next, she walked the 4 down the rail and straight into the corner. He realized she could run the game out, skunking him if he did not find a way to distract her. She was lining up the 1 ball for a cut in the side and sunk it.

"Question two: Why do you like the game of pool so much?"

"That one is easy. It is a game of sensuality and sexuality." *Smiling while lining up the 7 ball to drop into the corner pocket.* After she dropped the ball in the corner like planned, she ran her finger slowly and seductively across the rail. Her voice dropped an octave as she explained: "The rails are smooth like skin; the felt is soft and inviting while the cold slate behind it reminds you of strength and sturdiness. You get to use this long hard shaft," wrapping her hand around it and sliding it gently up and down, "to vary the speed and strength of the shot to manipulate these balls into doing exactly what you want them to do. The table itself a playground of seduction." Going back to her regular octave, "Sorry you asked? I really should come with a warning label."

Ari was thinking he damned sure did not need the visual; he was already picturing it as she spoke. Damn woman doesn't miss a beat. She hasn't shown any sign of embarrassment about any topic brought up so far. God, I hope an empath can't read minds. He is beginning to think he might be slightly out of his league. She was smart, fearless, and always gave well-thought-out answers to any question he has asked so far. She was brutally honest and fierce, a force to be reckoned with—which he found refreshing and unnerving at the same time.

She lined up that 1 ball to walk it to the corner in front of him. She made eye contact and watched his reaction. This time giving him a warm and friendly smile before sinking that ball. She only had the 8 ball left. She sized up the table and him, not real sure how to play this one out.

"Question three: Is being an empath difficult?"

Delaney miss-cued on the 8 ball. That cue ball didn't even come close. Then she shouted Mazy's name in her mind. What the hell would make her tell him about that? Just wait until next time she converses with her. Holy shit, this was going to take her a moment to figure out how to answer without sounding like a nutcase.

"Yes, more difficult than you can imagine. Mostly it's a curse, but every now and then, it's a gift. It doesn't make you popular because you can sense when others are lying to you or don't like you but say they do. You sense people's hidden thoughts and secrets. Certain people carry a lot of angst and negative energy, and you can't stomach to be around those people for very long. I have met many that try to portray a perfect Christian belief, and on the inside their soul is black with jealousy, anger, and hatred. Others freak out when you say something that you shouldn't know. You get years of counseling for anger management and sadness that you can't really explain because it didn't really belong to you. You have to wait for juvenile records to close so you can go in the military. You live your life at a distance because that is how you survive. I didn't even know what it was until I was an adult. I am marked; a palmologist told me once, but I didn't know what it meant. Both my palms are marked with Ms. M on one hand means highly intuitive and in tune with world; M on other palm means good fortune and good luck. To have both marked is rare. I made the mistake of telling a doctor to please not be sad; she was in a better place and back with his father. Next thing you know, someone has figured out what you are and want to run a bunch of tests. They literally cement wires all around your head, wanting to know what kind of things you dream, and desire, then try to dissect your life piece-by-piece. I have been called a freak and a witch by narrow-minded people who cannot grasp the concept of what an empath is. I got nicknamed the "Boo Hoo Box" because I cry during books, TV, or whatever else because I feel an emotional attachment too. God takes a select few and gives them an internal core strength to assist in carrying the world's emotional baggage, because apparently it is something you are born with, then gives you some kind of hidden honing device that draws people to you. Like right now I am overwhelmed with the sense of pity you feel for me and the guilt you feel for asking the question."

"I'm sorry, I can see how that would make things difficult. So when is it a gift?" *Almost afraid to ask because he doesn't want her to leave nor does he want to upset her anymore than he felt he has.*

He listened carefully as she spoke while he lined up his shot. He wanted to take his time fearing she was going to run out on him. Plus, she was literally kicking his ass on his own pool table; he had some catching up to do. He did not want to be skunked by her, and he knows the only thing that saved that from happening was question three.

"When your friend hears you, reminds her to put on her seatbelt a mile before she is in a roll-over accident with her new car and she escapes with nothing but a couple bruises and bumps. The same digital dash you saw in a dream months earlier and talked to her about it because it was weird and nobody had a dash like that you knew of. When you have a great Sergeant as a boss and you can feel something is not right, who lets you call home. Speak to your grandfather to find out your grandmother is going in for a routine surgery that you knew nothing about, intentionally I might add.

The minute I told him I was on my way home he knew what I felt. He told my grandmother how much he loved her and she was the best thing that ever happened to him, along with his children. After they rolled her into surgery, he went down to the chapel and prayed. Which I know sounds pretty normal except he was an agnostic/atheist since coming back from the war. He was praying my feelings were wrong; it was a simple surgery after all to remove a clot in her leg. My boss put me on emergency leave and let me head home. I was just outside of Chicago when it hit me. I called my boss and told her my grandmother had just died. She asked if my grandfather had called, and I had to inform her no, that he was about to find out. She was silent, knowing I was still 6 hours from home; she did agree to get the paperwork ready but wanted me to confirm when I got there." *Choking back the tears.* "My body was so overwhelmed with love and warmth, a feeling that it was going to be alright, that I had to pull over so that I could breathe. The worse part of the whole thing, I saw her fall in the archway by being in my grandfather's body, looking through his eyes, as he rounded the kitchen to help her up about a year before it happened in a dream. When I told them about the dream, my grandmother made me promise not to tell her anything else I saw about her. It was a promise I hated making. Doctors figured that fall had created the clot that eventually led to her death. It was a promise I never wanted to break so bad in my life. Had it been to anyone other than my grandmother, I would have."

"God, that must have been really hard to process. How was your boss when you confirmed what had happened?"

"She had made a note at the time I called, and it was within five minutes of the time of death they told my Grandfather and listed on her certificate. I think it made her uneasy. I had to explain to her how the dreams are the worst because they are impossible to decipher with certainty when I have them. I don't even try unless I have the same dream more than once. I know they are trying to tell me something important."

After he missed the 13 ball, it was all but over, this pool game. She was lined up on the 8 ball to the corner pocket. All he kept thinking was this was going to be the end to this night and he was not ready for her to go home yet. He rather enjoyed her honesty, and he could see how people find it incredibly easy to talk to her. He also could understand that distant vibe she gives off.

He tried imagining himself in her shoes for a minute and concluded there was no way he could handle it.

"I'll take that drink now. I think I need it."

Ari walked over to the mini fridge and looked to see what was in it. He offered her a beer or a coke. She opted for the beer. Then she called 8 ball to the corner pocket and smiled. Her smile is infectious even when it was a fore-warning as to something coming. It was when she put her finger to her mouth and "hmmm'd" it dawned on him that she was thinking about three questions to ask him. That was when his stomach started to do flip-flops. After the three he just asked her, he expected worse in return. He brought her the beer after opening it for her. She leaned her rear against the pool table taking a drink. All he could think was how beautiful she looked right now. He didn't know if it was her vulnerability at that moment or the fact that she was so different from anyone else he had ever know. She was sexy, tall, lean, and top-heavy, which was accentuated by that tight black T-shirt, but this beauty was way beyond physical attributes. Maybe she is a beacon of light that shines brightly.

"Ok question one: You are a fairly handsome man with a good heart. You seem to be well rounded. Why are you not married?"

"How do you know I am not?"

"Question with a question, cute and a little funny, but remember that honesty thing we agreed upon?" *Raising that one eyebrow yet again.*

"I was married. Aubrey. I met her in college, and we married shortly after. Your turn to rack by the way. I thought it would be happily ever after, didn't turn out that way. As my business grew along with the revenue it generated, I began thinking long term and starting a family. She never stopped thinking about prestige, fancy cars, credit cards, and bank accounts. She never wanted any children because then she would not be the center of attention. She liked being the center of attention all the time and especially liked the attention of men, never really caring how she got it. It got to a point where I decided I was not going to be sidelined in my own life. I brought Jamison in, my best friend, to be a partner in my business because we grew up together and went to the same college. Plus, he is an outstanding engineer. It was an added bonus that he didn't like her from day one, called her a gold-digging tramp, looking for a paycheck to latch onto. That helped because I knew he would not let me waiver in my decision to divorce her. My mother and father were married for a long time and loved each other through every change in life. I knew I could never have that with Aubrey. Every now and then she does something heinous to make my life hell. Like a woman I went on four dates with, she harassed her enough until the poor woman called me and said this just wasn't going to work for her. Intimidation is her tactic of choice."

Delaney laughed about the intimidation word. Mazy says she intimidates men, and she knows she really does. She is independent, secure about herself, comes off confident but is far from it.

"Sad, some people are just not good people deep in the soul. They feed the wrong wolf, and that becomes the strongest."

They kept taking their turns as he answered her questions.

"Question two: This is a beautiful house, filled with a lot of love. I don't ever remember seeing a for sale sign, and I always thought it was a shame because it is so welcoming. Which tells me you inherited it. Was it hard losing your parents and coming back here?"

"Ok, that might take me getting used to you doing that."

"What?"

"Knowing stuff like that without me telling you about it. Losing my parents was the worst thing I ever had to deal with. I was in college when I got a phone call from the State Police saying my parents were in a car crash. They were on their way back to Great Falls from here when they were hit head-on by a guy who fell asleep behind the wheel after a 15-hour shift. My father died at the scene; my mother lived long enough for me to arrive at the hospital. She had a lot of internal injuries and was in critical condition. I spoke to her for just a moment before she passed. She told me she was proud of the man I had become and she saw great things and an unimaginable love in my future. Then she apologized to me. That was hard. She told me that she will not go on alone without my father and that he was waiting for her. She told me one day I would spread my wings and soar to great heights. She inhaled for the last time and told me she loved me to the moon and back. Then the sirens of machines started going off, and I stood there frozen. My brain could not process what had happened. Jamison and his parents came and picked me up. My aunt, who used to take care of the house in my absence, helped me make the funeral arrangements. Coming back here was easy. You are right; this house is filled with tons of love. I used to slide down those stairs as a child. I grew up a couple years here before they bought a house in Great Falls. I still walk in the kitchen sometimes and wish I smelled the cookies she used to bake. My father loved his cookies so this house and the other one used to always have a sweet aroma that burned into your memory. I used to come home from college sometimes and take a bag of them back with me. I feel close to them here, and I feel most like myself here."

"Oh, I didn't sense some of that. A customer of mine a couple roads over told me how fond she was of your parents and how sad it was what happened to them. She never told me what had happened. Funny your mother used to say to the she loved you to the moon and back, I tell my son that all the time. They sounded like they were great parents.

"Alright, this last question will be less sad. What would ever make you think to ask me if I was a domme? That question seemed so off the cuff to me that my curiosity is running a muck."

Oh lord, he was so wishing it was his shot but alas it was not. He could feel his cheeks starting to blush with embarrassment. She stared at him waiting patiently for a second before taking her shot.

Honesty is the best policy with her. Swallow your pride and spill the beans. "That night at the bar, I was a little curious about you, so Jamison and I found your social media page. I researched it a couple times."

"Stalker! No just kidding, but that would explain where you would come up with a question like that. You know you can ask me anything; I rarely get embarrassed. I get self-conscious sometimes, but I almost never embarrass. I guess I will have to review what is on my social media page."

"Why would you get self-conscious? You are attractive, intellectual, and well spoken."

"I don't see what others see when they look at me. Most people are stimulated visually. For me on the other hand, all I do is feel, so my stimulation is more intellectually based. I can look at some of the best looking people and only sense the ugliness they hide."

Hmmm.

They played game after game exchanging questions and answers, observing each other the whole time. It seemed as if time were standing still. He did learn her husband died overseas when her son, Reese, was three. It had been just the two of them with help from her parents. She learned he had no siblings; Jamison was more family than blood allowed as a younger brother; they trudged the trenches together. She felt a little more secure in Reese's future as an only child after learning of Ari's path. She wasn't overwhelmed being in his presence; she found herself to be quite comfortable. She even played nice, not using any more power of persuasion to give him suggestive sexual thoughts or visuals.

She honed in on his statuesque frame, his quietly handsome and well chiseled features. His demeanor she found to be incredibly attractive. She noticed how his dark brown hair had just enough wave to give him a tussled look and cast shadows over his piercing eyes. Neither of them had any idea what time it was or how long they had been playing. They both seemed so comfortable with each other that it just didn't seem to matter.

"Can you show me a simple domme move without any pain?" he asked after the game had finished.

Well that interrupted her thoughts. Abrupt left turn. It took her but a moment to come up with something PG-rated that would not scare him and send him running for the hills. What he thought mattered to her, which was an odd sensation.

Ok, she thought she would play along. Curiosity might have killed the cat, but satisfaction brought it back, something her grandmother used to say. She moved him over to face the wall, but back about two feet. Then she faced him and kicked his feet apart a little further. Spinning around in front of him, she put her back against his chest and weaved her fingers between his. Gripping them tightly, she raised them up and jerked him forward into her, both leaning against the wall. He was taken by her strength for a moment and the speed of it all. Then he realized, he was the one more in a domme position than her. Her heart-shaped ass was resting up against his crotch. He could feel the blood start to flow. His chest was against her back feeling her every breath. Her heels had made her the same height as him until she leaned into the wall. She instructed him to glide his lips from her neck to her shoulder. When he did as instructed, he could feel every synapse firing in his brain at once: the way her hair smelled of coconut, her perfume was soft and flowery, and how her body temperature began to heat his. Every nerve ending in his body stood to attention waiting impatiently for the next command. Then she told him to gently nip her shoulder by the deltoid muscle. When he did, her head tilted back against his collarbone and an erotically soft moan escaped her lips. His body went haywire, envisioning the pure pleasure of very erotic sex with her. He needed to let go of her but seemed frozen in place. This does not happen to him ever! He has never touched a woman and envisioned sex. What the hell was going on? She causes his body and brain to react in an unfamiliar ways, and he is not sure he likes it, but he doesn't want to stop it either.

Then she began to lower his arms from the wall, still pressed against him, she glanced at his watch. 2:48 A.M.

"Oh my gosh, it's late, I have to go."

She released his hands and removed herself from in front of him, making her way over to her hoodie. Once she donned that, she walked back over to him and held her hand out in a handshake gesture. He was completely taken back by this. However, he did shake her hand.

"Thank you for a very enjoyable evening. I have to go because I do not want Reese to wake up and worry about me. Plus I still have a 30-minute drive home."

Before he could even get a "Thank you and we will have to do it again sometime" out of his mouth she was flying up the stairs and out the front door.

Ari stood there dumbfounded for a moment. That woman was always leaving his house like a whirlwind. A handshake instead of an attempt at a kiss goodnight, although he wasn't sure if he would have tried that if not for fear of her reaction, especially after what he just felt during a demonstration, but hell, she never even gave him the option. Luckily, all the balls were already in pockets so he only had to put the sticks back up on the wall and headed up to take a shower to try to calm himself a bit. His body was still reacting to her touch, fully charged. Shaking his head and thinking that woman is a fireball— a vigorous, energetic, luminous fireball. She put his head in a tailspin every time she entered or exited.

He got in the warm shower hoping to dissipate some of that energy she left him with. He started thinking about her sultry eyes and the way she looked at him before shooting a shot that would be a game changer. Her eyes were so expressive and unbelievably sexy. That warm water was nothing compared to her body against his. He wasn't one to think with anything other than his brain about women, so it had him flustered that his brain was betraying him this way. His brain was recalling every detail in technicolor for him, right down to the smell of her hair, the perfume she must have dabbed behind her ear, and that sexy little moan she did. That erotic moan shot straight to his cock. It took him a long time to fall asleep.

Delaney decided to call Mazy's cell phone, knowing she was still up, probably reading the new book she just bought. She was excited to talk to her.

Miranda starts singing ringtone.

Mazy answered, "Hello"

"Um, how much did you have to drink at the bar that night we ran into Ari and Jamison?"

"Not much, why?"

"You told Jamison about being an empath. Guess what Ari questioned me about?"

"Oh, I did. I am so sorry. I don't even know what possessed me to say it. They remember that word like you remember distracting. Well, Delaney you can't keep that secret your whole life. How will you ever let anyone get close to you keeping secrets? What do you mean he questioned you? About being an empath on your date?"

"Not a date, although it kind of felt like a very comfortable date. I have to admit, once I got past the tough questions, I had a really nice time. One of his questions was about being an empath. We were playing pool for questions and answers. I learned a lot about him. His parents died in a horrible car crash, which broke my heart. Oh, and apparently I have to check my page to see what the hell kind of domme crap I got on there because he thinks I hide whips and chains. I guess the two of them checked that out to try to figure out what kind of person I was. I imagine his risk assessment business makes him naturally good at research so I might want to refresh my memory as to what they were looking at."

Mazy is laughing her ass off.

"Oh shit that is hilarious. He thinks you are some dominatrix, with a hidden empath power, who likes whips and chains, oh and intimidates the hell out of men. You gotta admit that is frickin' funny as hell. Are you going to call him?"

"Crap, I don't have his number and didn't think to get it. That didn't even register in my brain. I saw the time and grabbed my sweatshirt and hauled ass out the door."

"Did you give him your number? No wait, I already know the answer to that one. Delaney Marie Delisle, you are an asshole. A nice man showed you a good time, and your escape and evade ass did what you always do, RUN! I think this one might surprise you. I think he might work at finding a second date, then what are you going to do, huh?"

"You know I hate it when you call me by my full name; it reminds me of something my mother does when she is cross with me. I don't know what I will do; I am not a physic. Besides, he may not, because he asked me to show him a domme move."

"Now we are getting somewhere; you didn't let your freak fly, did you?"

"Not exactly, I made him the domme, but when I touched him that was a whole different story. You know I don't usually touch people because of what I might feel or see, but when I touched him, the surge that pulsed through my body was intoxicating. Once I locked my fingers into his, visions of ecstasy began to flow like a raging river. I could feel every bit of his body against mine. It was a perfect fit. I could feel that fire ignite in my lower abdomen. Desire started rushing through every one of my veins. God, I was so consumed by it, I almost lost my damn bearings. When he bit my shoulder I began to shudder like you do right before you have an orgasm; it was insanity. Then I looked at his watch and bolted out the door like a crazy woman."

"You know I fucking hate you right now. Visions of hot, steamy sex leading to orgasms, yep, I fucking hate you at this moment. Well, this romance novel is ruined for me. Then you ran like you always do. So answer me this, was he at least a good kisser?"

"Um," *a silent pause*, "I don't know. I saw his watch, shook his hand, and bolted so I could get home."

"Laney, what the hell is wrong with you? You had an awesome time, and you shook the man's hand like a nun. I am so disappointed in you right now. Visions of what could be and you shook his damn hand; plus, he can't even call you for another date. You are an asshole; you are my best friend but you are an asshole. He sounded like he was a pretty good match all the way around. I can hear your happiness, and I know you were smiling when you talked about him. It sounded like you found his conversation stimulating, and you were there quite a while. Where did you go by the way? Never mind, it don't really matter. You had a good time then you ran like usual—oh, but not before shaking the man's hand. You better hope he don't try to contact me for more information 'cause I might do something crazy like give him your damn phone number. Hell, I might even tell him where you live. You slay me. Opportunity doesn't knock every day, ya know. Right now, I just want to jump in my car and come over to kick your ass. You are such a dumbass sometimes. I love you to death, but sometimes you are a dumbass"

"I know, and I think I might regret running this one off a bit. He is really nice, and I don't feel overwhelmed or uptight around him. I am not real sure what I feel around him. I damn sure know what I felt when I touched him; I got damp panties as proof. I am not going to sleep a wink tonight. I hear you, but he is swimming laps around in my head. Maybe I will give him my number next time I drop him off a package. I don't usually do things like that though, so I will just have to see."

"You better give him your number, or I swear to God, I will. You like him and God knows you haven't let anyone get that close to you in a long time. What do you always say? Sex is easy; it's the communication part of a relationship that is hard. He sounds like all communication at the moment, but that can change. Besides, what if his sex is like what you saw and felt?"

"Damn it, Mazy, I have to try to sleep tonight and that is already going to be difficult. I will admit that he was a perfect gentleman, until I touched him and made him come out of his comfort zone."

"Laney, let's be realistic. You don't just knock people out of their comfort zone; you bulldoze their asses out it. One day I swear you are going to meet your match, when you least expect it. I just can't wait to watch it all unfold like my next great romance novel. Ya know I love you like a sister and I hate seeing you alone. I used to think you were too damn picky, but I do know it is not as easy for you; you have extenuating circumstances that do not make relationships easy. I hear you tell me how hard it is to love you all the time, but I know you also make that difficult by holding yourself back because of your gift."

"Awe, I love you too, girl. You know I would probably lose my mind if you didn't keep me grounded. Well, I am home now and I should probably shower and try to get some sleep. I didn't want Reese to worry if he woke up and I wasn't here, even though he knew I was going to play pool. I will talk to you more tomorrow. Night."

Delaney went in, took a shower, and laid on her bed thinking about her evening with Ari. Her thoughts were all over the place and out of control. Sex popped in there a few times, but mostly it was about the conversations they had. She truly enjoyed the conversations. She recapped most of them in her head like a picture show with remote, rewind, play again, and repeat. She did try to steer away from how his body felt next to hers, which had a strange turn-on quality to it. That was just overstimulation that she was not ready to think about at this time. Hell, she was still reeling from actually going through with the date in the first place. Wait, did she just call it a date? Damn, she is tired and needs to let her brain rest.

CHAPTER 4

*J*amison waited until 8:30 A.M. before calling Ari to grill him as to how his date went. Jamison told him he sounded a bit giddy, like a young school girl, after listening to him for a while. At least until they got to the empath topic. Jamison had mixed emotions about what it could mean for his friend. He even asked how she could deal with all that and not lose her mind. Ari tried to explain how she goes deep into herself to deflect it thanks to some counseling and military training; at that point, he realized he was no better at explaining it than she was the night before. Besides, she said it doesn't happen all the time. When he got to the domme move, Jamison almost fell out of his chair. He was floored by the fact that Ari asked her to show him one, found it hilarious that she made him the domme, and was on the edge of his chair listening to Ari's reactions to all of it. He was seeing an all new side of Ari he didn't know even existed and was thrilled that his best friend was so full of life on the other end of the phone. He missed that part of his friend.

"Arousal was an understatement. It was beyond crazy. I felt fire, passion, excitement, nervousness, romance, kink, and heat all rolled up into this fireball named Delaney. We both know I have never been one to let my penis do the thinking, but when she touched me, my brain saw mind-blowing sex and my body was all about it. She is a vortex of energy that sweeps you up and carries you with her. She has the most expressive eyes I have ever seen, while in my core I haven't seen anything yet. I feel there is so much more to come. Then she left in a whirlwind just like she did the first time we met her. No kiss, no phone number, nothing but a handshake."

"So let me get this straight, you did *not* kiss her, even get her phone number, you didn't give her yours, and have no scheduled plans for another date but yet you want her. Now what the hell are you going to do about that? She doesn't flirt at work because she takes her job seriously, and God only knows next time she'll be at your place. I am so *not* asking her friend Mazy for yet another favor—I think I tapped that well dry. What are you going to do?"

"I don't know yet. The only thing I know for sure is I am going to send her flowers at work Monday. I have been going over what the colors mean, and there is no color that represents I had a great time and would like to do it again sometime. Yellow is out of the question because I am *not* looking to be thought of by her as just a friend. I think not on the dreaded friend zone, argh. I may not know where this could end up, but I know I don't want to be trying to fight my way out of the friend zone, for a fact."

"God, the friend zone; that is like a kiss of death to us men. Well, you can always ask her friend Mazy for help. Technically, you haven't asked her for anything yet. I was the one who pumped her for info and then again to get you a way in. Yep, I think it is your turn. Prep yourself because she is blunt and has the mouth of a sailor. She is about as straight forward as they come."

"You're right, women talk. I figure if she tells me to piss off than it's likely that Delaney would not like to entertain the idea of doing that again. If she helps me, well then I am going to pursue it. Mazy is the one person she communicates with often; I know that from last night. I heard Mazy mentioned at least half a dozen times. She will either help me or she won't."

After getting off the phone with Jamison, Ari jumped on the computer and opened Delaney's social media page. He used her page to navigate to Mazy's page. He then sent Mazy a message and made a mental note that her page listed her phone number and address; however, Delaney's did not. He checked out her page for a couple minutes and realized just how different the two of them are. It did not take long for Mazy to reply back to him with Delaney's address and a reminder to be kind to her friend. Then he thought about how to show her his appreciation for the help she gave him. He sent back a kind message in return but just didn't feel like it was enough.

Monday morning, Ari got up and called the flower shop. He had thought about what to say on the card most of the evening, once he decided he was for sure sending flowers. He didn't want it to say too much or too little. The woman on the phone had been very helpful. Her solution to the meaning of the colors problem was brilliant. He wanted something special for the most colorful woman he has ever had the acquaintance of meeting. The florist recommended the kaleidoscope rose. It was beyond perfect.

—✵—

Today seemed exhausting for Delaney. She was hot, tired, covered in newspaper ink, and now she had to go home and pull her car up on the ramps in the garage. She wanted to see if she could figure out why her car has a spongy feeling every now and then. It was just turning out to be one of those Mondays you know you should have just stayed in bed. The only thing she had going for her was the fact that she started today's dinner yesterday; with Reese having practice, she did not want to feel crazy rushed.

Delaney finally pulled into the office and unloaded the car. She heard Shelby cooing the minute she noticed it was her. She could not quite make out what she was saying with trays pressed against her face. *Dear God, please don't let it be about another man she thinks I should meet.* Delaney walked up the center aisle and went to turn into her case when she saw them. Sitting on her desk were two-dozen rainbow colored roses. Delaney set down her trays and just stared at them for a moment. They were the most vibrant colors she has ever seen; the blues and purples caught her attention the most. Then she read the card: *After women, flowers are the most lovely thing God has given the world,* a quote he found online.

"They arrived for you this afternoon. Are they not the most beautiful roses? I don't know who he is, but he has exquisite taste in flowers, and that is the most romantic quote. Every customer that has noticed them today has commented about them, and they smell divine. Awe, I'm envious."

Delaney finished putting up her stuff and tried to figure out a way to get them home safely. She grabbed a box out of the recycling and set the large glass vase down in it. Then she packed some bubble packing around it. She did not want it to break on that thirty-minute ride home. She had a little trouble getting it in the car. It was so large, it barely fit on her passenger seat, and it filled her car with that sweet rose smell. She carried them very carefully into the house and placed them in the center of the kitchen table. She read that card at least three times since bringing them home.

Reese helped guide his mother up on the ramps after school. Once secure on there, Delaney got out and retrieved the creeper. She also grabbed a flashlight. Reese was all about teasing his mom a bit about the flowers and her pool game date until she sent him to go and get the mail. She reminded him to get Nana's as well and drop hers off there. He gladly jumped on the ORV and raced to the boxes. When he got to the end of the driveway, there was a gentleman in a car there looking lost. Reese noticed him looking at his phone then the numbers on the boxes.

When he noticed Reese, he unrolled the window. "Excuse me, I am looking for someone, can you help me? Her name is Delaney."

"You found the place; give me a moment to grab the mail and make one stop then I will take you back."

Reese grabbed the mail and put it in between the seats, whipped a U-turn, and headed back the way he had just come from. Ari followed him up the drive until the ORV stopped at a house about 300 feet in. The young man held up one finger and ran the mail into the house.

"Who is that?" asked Nana.

"If I had to guess, I think it is Mom's pool game date from the other night. From her conversations with Mazy, she rather enjoyed herself. If the huge bouquet of multi-colored roses on the kitchen table is an indication, I would guess he enjoyed himself as well."

"Nice. I can't remember a time she ever invited someone who wasn't a family friend here. He must be something special, rare if your mother is entertaining. Well, don't keep the man waiting. Show him on back."

Reese came out of the house and waved to the man to follow him. They went back maybe half a mile down a two-track through some pines before coming to a clearing. It was in that clearing that the picture became clear; he had seen her building something on her media page. The something she was building was a very different type of house. It looked like stone until you got close then it looked like wood, firewood to more precise. It was just as unique as her.

"Who shall I tell her is calling on her?"

"Ari, Ari Van Ash," as he could not help but stare at the house and the way it blended in with nature because it was nature. He could see a sunroom attached to the lower half, while the upper half had a balcony that wrapped around the one end. He was having trouble staying on the young man's heels because the house was distracting until they came into the garage.

"Reese, will you roll that flashlight back under here?" Her voice muffled from under the car when she heard him come back into the garage. The damn thing tried to go AWOL on me."

"Hey, Mom, Ari Van Ash is here to see you."

Delaney startled forward and banged her forehead into the skid plate. She tried to recover by asking him to wait just a moment while she finished up. She shined the light all around the suspension and did not see anything that would cause her a spongy feeling. She also stalled a bit to figure out how to handle Ari being there by pulling on some of the suspension. *Damn you, Mazy.* She was in her garage clothes (stained basketball shorts and a t-shirt), under her car, and now sporting a slight goose egg on her forehead. After a few moments of contemplating, it was time to face the music. She came rolling out from under the car. Reese helped her off the creeper, smiling a shit-eating grin the whole time, while Ari just watched. *Yep, just how every woman wants to be seen by a man under the car, dirty, while her smart-ass son beams with joy at her embarrassment and discomfort.*

"What are you doing here?"

"Before you answer that, Ari, um, can I have some dinner before I have to go to practice?" Reese asked.

Delaney looked at her watch and thought, *Oh, crap.* She had about 45 minutes to finish dinner and get him fed before Jay and his mom arrived to pick him up for practice. Plus, Ari was standing in her garage, and she was still waiting to hear why he was there.

"I hope you are hungry; follow me." *Directed to both of them.*

Coming through the garage led straight into the kitchen. Delaney washed her hands and her face after Reese gave her the finger point to his forehead. Then she turned the oven on broil and uncovered the rice. She added a bit more water and used a screen over it to steam some broccoli. Reese motioned

Ari over to the kitchen table to have a seat. Informing him of what was for dinner tonight. Ari noticed the very unique kitchen table. It was three slats of trees and the gaps were filled with pennies, rocks, and what looks like acrylic. He also noticed the flowers sitting in the center of it; the kaleidoscope roses were perfect.

"You guys want to wash up for dinner. Reese, why don't you show Ari where the restroom is."

Ari followed Reese down a hallway that had pictures hanging on the wall. He saw one with Delaney standing with a Colonel (he knew the rank because his uncle was one) and three men with stars on their collars before entering a bathroom with a hunting décor. Even the glass-enclosed shower had a camo background and deer motif. A pop of hunter orange was sprinkled throughout but was kept even toned by the use of different shades of browns in the linens. It was very hard not to be in awe and find it humorous at the same time; it was a manly bathroom in a single woman's house. Nature statues held the soap and other toiletries. As he came back down the hall, the smell of dinner was teasing him. He didn't even realize how hungry he was.

She set down a plate of food in front of each of them. Then she got Reese some milk as preferred and Ari a water as preferred before having a seat at the table with her dinner. She noticed Ari looking at the table intently.

Ring Ring. Talking through the machine: *Oh my God, Laney, the most beautiful bouquet of flowers came for me today. I accused the poor deliveryman of having the wrong address until he said my name. That man, Ari, sent me a dozen yellow roses with the sweetest card. It's not signed with anything but an A, but I know it was him. Oh yeah, don't be mad, I gave him your address. Funniest thing, my husband saw them, and that idiot thinks they are from you for whatever latest project I helped you with. I think he thinks the A stands for Army strong. He is such a dumbass. This one might finally make you put those running shoes away. I think he liked your pool game date a lot. I hope you are not still pissed about the whole empath thing. Love you, call me when you get this!*

"Awkward, guess you should have broke dinner tradition and answered that one, huh, Mom?" *Snickering at her from across the table while Ari raised one eyebrow mouthing the word "running shoes?"* All Delaney could do was smirk back at Reese and shove a piece of chicken in her mouth.

"Dude, you keep staring at that table, and your dinner is going to get cold. Mom and Mazy built it. Are you looking for your birth year penny? That is what most people do. If you don't like the smothered chicken you can slide it over here."

"Reese, be polite to guests. You know what it is like when people see the house for the first time. Besides, there is more chicken in the oven. Sorry, teenage boys think with their stomachs and their legs are hollow."

"No need to apologize, he is right. I have been distracted since I pulled up. This house, the table, this outstanding dinner has me on sensory overload. I was sitting here trying to figure out how you made it and why the pennies."

"Pennies in the table was Mazy's idea to match my kitchen countertops, and people just seem to find it fun looking for a specific year. The slats are from a tree that stood alone in the clearing that I thought had unique markings when we cut it down to build. My dad's friend sliced it into four slats; three make up the table and the fourth is part of a bench in the gazebo. The rocks are river rocks. I built a frame, and then we poured a clear acrylic resin over it until we had the desired thickness. It has a few flaws, but I like it and that is what matters most. This place is my sanctuary. But I am sure you did not drive all this way to discuss my table; you never did say what you were doing here."

"You rushed out of my house so quick the other night, I never got to invite you and your son to a paintball challenge. This weekend, one of my clients is hosting a private challenge and cookout to celebrate his facility being listed as one of the top rated. Jamison and I got invited because our risk assessment saved him thousands in insurance and design changes helped his course to be one of the best. I heard you like to shoot and thought you might enjoy it; after seeing the bathroom, I think that was a fair assessment."

"Please say yes, Mom, please, please. Hunting you would be so much fun, plus I need opportunity to catch up. You kind of smoked me last time we played."

Just then she heard Jay coming through the front door, saved by the buddy.

"Yo, Reese, you ready? Oh, other mother dinner smells great. I hope you saved me some." *As he grabs a piece of chicken off Reese's plate and pops it in his mouth.*

"I'll pack you a to-go box you can take home after practice."

Reese jumped up from the table, walked over, and kissed his mom on the head telling her he loved her plus he would do his dishes when he got home tonight. Then he exited just like she does. He grabbed his gym bag, and poof, he was gone in a whirlwind. Must be a family trait.

Shouting on his way out the door, "Hunting you would be fun, just saying, Mom. Think hard about it. Love you to the moon and back. Later."

"I know that sounded funny. I taught him some escape and evade tactics, and last time we played paintball, I shot him, a few times. He just wants to see if his skills have advanced and if he can get some revenge. I know my son would love for his friend Jay to come as well; you know they are like two peas in a pod. If we could make that happen then I am definitely in."

Delaney and Ari finished eating and then she gave him a tour of the house. The sunroom was interesting with bottles in the wall that glistened in the sunlight and lit up the room. The concrete floor was covered in glow-in-the-dark paint. He learned those walls are 16 inches thick which would explain why he didn't hear the car pull up. The house itself was warm. He listened to her about the details. Affordability was the main reason she built it, but its ability to block the world out was incredible. The only thing she feels in this house is what is inside of this house. He understood why she called it a sanctuary.

When they got to the hall of pictures, he learned a lot. Those stars were her bosses; the Colonel was an aide. He figured she did some unusual stuff in the military by the way she avoided specifics. He had seen one picture of Reese's father who was also in the Army when he died. The two pictures he was most drawn to were one of her and Reese making a heart with their hands and one of her with odd streaks of light across the entire picture. He even asked what caused it; she had no idea. She thought it may have been sunlight reflecting off jewelry, but she wasn't wearing any. He studied her face for a moment, and then he reached and cupped her cheeks in his hands. He leaned forward and kissed her with a hunger he had never felt before. He couldn't help himself. He wanted to see if those full lips were as soft as they looked. He knew not to ask in fear of her possible rejection. From his conversation with Mazy, it was all or nothing with her. Don't give her the opportunity to run.

Her mouth was hot, sweet tasting, and those lips were soft. He let his hands move from her face to trail a finger down each of her arms. Surprising even himself, he grabbed her wrists and raised them above her head, moving her until her back was against the wall. His hard chest pressing into her soft breasts. Those expressive eyes of hers popped open then lowered again when he removed his lips from hers and placed soft kisses to her neck. He was taking her in until she was all his body wanted and could handle. Her breath hitched, her head tilted back, and she let out a soft, oh so sexy moan. He held her wrists with one hand and brought his free hand to the back of her hair, gripping it as gently as possible while pulling her into him. Then he nipped her collarbone skin, suckling it lightly afterwards. She was breathing heavily. Then he kissed his way back up to her lips. He knew he had to stop himself. He does not want a one night stand with this woman. Although, not completely sure what he does want with her. It took every ounce of will power to pull back and let her go. Hopefully, before she feels where all the blood rushing through his body is heading. He could have sworn that the room temperature raised at least 10 degrees.

"I should be leaving now. I wouldn't want to wear out my welcome."

He started to head back toward the kitchen when he spotted her cell phone on the counter. He picked it up and punched in his number calling himself. When he looked back up at her, she was still standing in the same spot he left her, looking confused, bewildered, and still trying to catch her breath. He had to leave her in the whirlwind she always leaves him in.

"Now you have my number and I have yours," *tapping his ringing pocket*. "Don't be afraid to use it. Dinner was delicious, and you must let me return the favor soon. I enjoyed meeting your son and touring your very unique home."

Turning on his heel, he headed out the same garage door he came in from. On his way out, he noted how many tools were in the garage and thought about how long she had been so independent. He instantly pictured her with a manual reading how to fix whatever she had to. For some reason this made him smile, a female grease monkey. It wasn't until he was driving home did it dawn on him that that stunt he just miraculously pulled off could backfire on him. He began losing all the confidence he felt while in her presence. He was still trying to figure out what made him behave animalistic like that in the first place. He was usually a gentleman when it came to women. At the moment, all he can think about is how uncomfortable his hard-on is making his slacks feel and why does he have a hard-on from just a kiss. He had kissed women in the past and that didn't happen. What the hell is she doing to him? Right before he stole that first kiss, he felt manly, hungry for her, confident, and powerful. He was surprised he would even have that reaction since her voice, her expressions, her eyes, and her presence in general acknowledge truth, honesty, and softness.

"Oh, that voodoo you do, is doing something to me." *He chuckled to himself for coming up with that.*

He thought about those soft full lips and how sweet her kiss was. That sexy little moan of hers was going to drive him insane. It was the second time he has heard it and could handle hearing it more. God, and the way her body felt pressed to his, her breasts against his chest. Her copper-colored tan skin beneath his lips. Yep, a cold shower was first thing on the agenda as soon as he gets home.

———

Delaney stood there for a second trying to regain her composer. It took a moment for her heart to stop trying to pound its way out of her chest and her breathing to return to normal. His kiss just rocked her to the core. A sharp, wanting ache began to throb between her legs, and she could hardly catch her breath. Another few minutes of that and her panties would not have stood a chance. His kiss tasted pure, a little animalistic maybe, but pure. She sensed nothing. That was very unusual for her, to sense nothing. No pain, no secret lies, no hidden agenda buried in that kiss. Just pure honesty and passion laced within.

She finally regained enough of her senses to grab the phone and give Mazy a call back. Oh, did she have a bone to pick with her. They talked for at least an hour while Delaney did the dishes. She had forgotten Reese would do them when he got home. All she could focus on was the effect his kiss had on her and how he invited them to paintball. His kiss was hungry yet soft. "It devoured me and threw me for a loop." Plus she pointed out how he just dommed her off instincts. Delaney had to tell her to quit laughing about four times. The fourth time was when Mazy reminded her that Reese usually does the dinner dishes. They talked about the car and possibly having to take it to a mechanic. Mazy snorted a laugh when Delaney told her about how Ari picked up her cell phone and called himself to get her number. Both women laughed when Mazy reminded her if she had password protection on her phone that couldn't have happened.

"Oh my God, imagine the shocked look on his face when he reads your number. Did he look at it?"

"Nope, he let his ring from inside his pocket." Delaney was in tears laughing so hard along with Mazy.

"Are you going to call him?"

"I have to; he didn't tell me where paintball was, and Reese is all about that paintball thing. He gets an opportunity to test his skills and hunt Mom."

"Good Lord, Delaney, don't you scare that man off. I know you well enough to know how you are once a weapon is placed in your hand. Don't go sniper commando on him. Take it easy on the poor man. He seems really nice."

"I'll do my best."

Knowing Mazy was right. She had no plans of not being herself. It was not her fault that people underestimate her. She was trained in weaponry. It also was not her fault she was a pretty good shot; that just came naturally.

She had called him. Oh, how she wished she could have seen the look on his face when the number came up. She laughs about it because she tried to get it changed, but the carrier would have no part of it, so now she just tells people it's a forewarning as a joke and just accepts it is what it is. They talked well into the night a couple of times about anything and everything. They both just seemed very comfortable with each other. Reese had even poked a little fun at her about it, mimicking kissy face and damsel fluttering eyes. He was really happy for his mom but was not about to miss an opportunity to tease her.

Saturday morning, the boys were very excited about paintball. They were decked out in hunting camo and ready to go. Both boys beat her to the truck in their excitement. They talked about defensive plans and offensive strategies during the hour and a half drive. Once they arrived they saw Ari and Jamison dressed similar. She had to admit Jamison looked very out of his element and a little uncomfortable. Worse of all, she could only look at him and think there was her first victim. She really could not help herself; she just has a mean streak is what her mother calls it. They gathered and listened to the rules, as Mr. Gillis explained them. Then each individual went to a table to pick out a face mask, chest protector, and gun filled with 200 paintballs.

"This is the US Army Alpha Black Elite; it packs a punch so do not aim for the head or face if possible. Your gear is to be worn at all times for your safety. This is a timed game of elimination. You have no friends out here. This is a ten-acre heavy wooded course filled with shacks and obstacles here and there for ambush and hiding use. The first horn will sound, and you have ten minutes to find a position on the course that works best for you. The second horn sound begins the elimination. The last horn will sound thirty minutes later meaning the end of the game. Shooting at those coming in will not be tolerated. Play nice and God have mercy on your souls. When everyone is geared up and checked we will begin." The instructor reminded her of a drill sergeant she had in basic training.

Jamison was struggling with the chest plate when Reese went over to help him after informing the instructor his mother needed pink paintballs pointing toward her. It's her favorite color.

"Now listen, I like you guys so here is the deal. Mom is going to run to the farthest area of the course, and then she will double back and start looking to pick us off one-by-one. Find a good hiding place, stay low, and think like a hunter and not the prey. She is military trained, a good shot, and really enjoys this kind of stuff. Your best hope is to stick together. That is Jay's and my plan. We will watch each other's back. She will move in the tree line and use the shadows as cover. She is sneaky as a fox and not afraid to get dirty. Watch the shadows." He finished getting Jamison adjusted and protected before walking back to Jay. Try not to get shot and good luck."

"Great, you got me out here with assassin Annie," Jamison scoffed at Ari. "Thanks, brother, and what the hell has she taught that kid? Saddest part, I am about to follow that teenager's advice because he sounds like he knows what he is talking about. I am thinking she has taught him some military tactics and survival skills."

Ari listened to every word Reese said. When that first horn sounded, he and Jamison took off running. They had lost sight of Delaney about a minute after the horn went off. She ran straight ahead, and then she was gone in the crowd of about thirty people playing. Ari noticed Jay and Reese exited to the right at some point. He and Jamison decided to head to the left. They both agreed on not hiding in the shed they came across but about 50 feet or so behind it. Then they heard the dreaded second horn. Jamison was probably the most nervous; hell, he had never even been out hunting before. How did he let Ari talk him into this?

Delaney had found her first victim. Some fellow player had decided to use one of the shacks as cover. From the tree line Delaney had the perfect shot. *I am beautiful, I am strong, I am a badass.* She lined up her sights, and once she breathed out she squeezed the trigger. Pink splattered all over the player's chest protector. Really frickin' pink, now she was just irritated. She ran to the player and used the shack as cover while she scanned the playing field. Then moving back to the tree line, running from shadow to shadow, she found another victim. She fired and took him out. It took her about fifteen minutes to find Ari and Jamison. Ari was crouched low, and she had to low crawl to get into position. Jamison was a much easier target. He was looking around all nervously and moving his body around a lot. She aimed at Ari first. Taking her time aiming and waiting for just the right moment, she let it rip. That paintball splattered right over his heart on the chest plate. Jamison was so surprised he moved exactly how she predicted he would. Two more rounds incoming. One hit to each side of his chest plate. If she could have shot three more she would have given him a smiley face. Then she moved out because she had an idea where Jay and Reese might have been hiding. It was somewhere she might have hidden.

Once she found them she had to admit she was kind of proud of the both of them. She had to low crawl into position and stay in a prone hold to line up a shot at them. Jay was in the shed as the lookout. He used brief glances to watch all around the shed. It took her a moment to realize Reese was on top of the shed. He was sniping whatever his lookout saw. Jay was relaying info to Reese. She watched as Reese aimed the barrel of his gun off the roof to line up the shot on someone Jay noticed. He directly hit his victim. She was proud of their teamwork but not so proud she wouldn't take a shot at either of them easily.

She stayed in the prone position and watched how often Jay was looking out. He was looking out about every minute for about ten seconds and switching sides. She figured he was looking out the other window as well when he was not visible to her. She remembered the instructor saying no head shots which limited her because that was all Jay was showing. *Clever boys, tricky, tricky, tricky.* Then she figured out she would hit the shack. God help her, she loved him like a son, but she was still going to shoot him. She lined up, and the moment he poked his head up to look around, she breathed out and nailed the shed with the paintball. Pink splattered all over his face mask. She heard him say something to Reese, and about two seconds later paintballs were hitting the ground all round her. Very clever boy, she could not help but smile. Then she heard the grass moving up behind her. She rolled over, sat up, and took aim on someone coming from her rear. Straight to the chest then quickly back down. It was seconds before paintballs were hitting all around her again. One landed about two inches from her shoulder. She knew Jay and Reese had locked in on her position. Damn, she had to move. She rolled to the right, waited a second, and rolled to the right again. She hoisted up on her elbows and realized she could not get a clear shot on Reese. She could only see the barrel of the gun; he was keeping his head low and blind shooting at her from Jay's directions. She spent about thirty more seconds watching and waiting before the third horn went off. She was thrilled and disappointed. She got Jay but couldn't get Reese. The three of them came in together laughing about all of it. She commended the boys on what a great job they did. Jay was a little disappointed because he figured he took on shrapnel, but Delaney assured him about his outstanding abilities because that was the only shot he gave her.

Jamison was much more relaxed during the cookout, poking fun at Delaney about folks with pink polka dots on their clothing. They ate and socialized, having a blast. Delaney noticed two young ladies talking to Ari and Jamison and pointing in her and Reese's direction. She figured they looked about Reese's age and were probably asking about him. He was a good-looking dishwater blond with her grey eyes, but she might be a little biased.

Most of the men there did not talk to Delaney, which he made a mental note of. She was smiling and playing tag with some of the smaller kids there. He started thinking about her wallflower comment and how she could go unnoticed and was perfectly good with that.

The instructor even came over to Delaney talking about her and her son giving some female JROTC cadets some extra assistance because he was tired of seeing them get taken out by the boys all the time. He figured her prior military background would help them immensely. He thought the girls needed confidence and some skills that would help build that confidence and who better to help them than a woman with Delaney's skills. She gave him her number and email, telling him she would be glad to help. With the party starting to wind down, Delaney gathered the boys for their hour and a half ride back. The boys were on cloud 9 still from that 30 minutes of play. Jay and Reese recapped the whole event the entire ride home. They would have to play again sometime because Reese wants to get his mom just once in his lifetime, but for now he was quite content with her not being able to get him this time and only wounding Jay per say. They had both survived.

———

It wasn't until Ari and Jamison were riding back that Jamison pointed out how Delaney had shot Ari in the heart, like an assassin cupid. Both men laughed but a little wary about those specific set of skills she seems to possess, which lingered in the back of both their brains. Ari had told Jamison about the picture he had seen, and when he asked her about what she did in the Army, she was very vague in her answers. "She tells me she was a secretary to some high ranking officials."

"Since when are secretaries trained like assassins?" It made both men silently wonder about what she might have really done in the Army. She was fierce on the paintball course without a doubt; plus she handled a weapon with no fear, and Reese told them when she was really angry or needs to clear her head she took a .45 to the back forty and obliterated a target, usually the head or heart. Reese had joked about never playing some buck hunter game with her because she head shots the biggest bucks and takes all the points but play COD with her because she sucks and can't figure out how the remote works. Both men agreed that if they ever played teams she was not allowed on anyone else's but theirs. It was safer that way, at least for them. Ari asked Jamie if he had noticed how hardly any men talked to her. Jamison laughed and said why would they, Assassin Annie is intimidating just like her friend Mazy warned about. Most men are afraid of a woman like that and with good reason. Why wouldn't they be? Confident, smart, and can hit a moving target. All women can bleed for a week and not die; they already have a built in scare tactic, but she definitely has some extras.

"She don't scare me of course, but I am not trying to date her either. Sorry, man, but I am thinking don't piss her off. I did notice the kids liked her a lot."

Both men chuckled thinking about her covered in dirt playing peek-a-boo around the trees and tables.

He called her later that evening to thank her for going and to invite her for dinner Sunday to repay the meal she had cooked for him, even when she didn't know she was going to have a guest. That thought made him laugh to himself. Again, she never skipped a beat. She often jokes about learning to adapt and overcome; he figures she has mastered that skill. He thought about her describing herself as a wallflower. He just couldn't see it. He had even asked Jamison if he would have noticed her. Jamison had thought a while before answering at his house that first day yes he would have noticed her, but in a club she would not have stood out to him. Ari couldn't understand the logic behind his answer because he believes he would notice her anywhere. He realized he likes when she is around; he laughs and he lives, truly lives. He had to admit to him-self that paintball would not normally be his forte, but he had a pretty good time. She has a strange effect on him that he just can't figure out. He could know her a lifetime and still discover something new about her all the time, thinking he will never truly know everything about her. She was different, very different from any other woman he had ever known, and he feels himself being pulled to her deep within his soul. She is a multi-level hurricane.

———∾———

Saturday morning, Reese and Delaney headed to the truck to get on their way to Great Falls. He thought it was strange that his mother made him grab a bunch of dimes and put them in his pocket. He had never seen his mom teach tactics to anyone else besides him and his friends. He figured this was going to be quite the experience for him.

They arrived at the paintball field to see the instructor standing with a group of young ladies. There were eight of them looking at her a little scared and definitely lacking some confidence, all dressed in old Army battle dress uniforms (BDUS). She did not see any of the parents, which she thought was a little odd.

"My name is Delaney Delisle, and this is my son Reese. I know I only get a couple hours so let's start with a couple questions. How many of you are afraid of the weapons?" About half raised their hands. "How many of you are afraid of getting shot?" All the girls' hands flew up. "Good, I can work with that. If you would please, Mr. Gillis, show us to the weapons."

They all walked back to the tables where he had 8 paintball guns and 12 face shields laid out.

"If I could have each of you get a spot on the table and put on a face shield. I want to see how well you shoot." While the girls were doing as instructed, Delaney was telling them statistically women are a much better shots then men are. She also told them how all women in Israel that are capable serve in the Israeli Army. The instructor had hung paper targets on a pulley rope 50 feet back like she asked the girls could see. Then she asked Reese for the dimes. He handed her a handful of them.

"Ok, ladies, this next part might feel a little funny, but I want you all to repeat after me. I am beautiful, I am strong, I am a badass." A couple of the girls giggled. "I want to wake up those inner warriors that you all hide inside and I know each of you have one. Say it again and mean it. You can yell it. You can say it inside your head." One of the girls yelled it, which surprised the others. "Good." Delaney walked over to her and asked her name.

"Abby, well Abigail, but they call Abby." Delaney picked up Abby's gun and showed them how to hold it on the table then had them do it. She helped a couple place their elbows and hands. Then she balanced the dimes on the barrels. Knowing if the dimes fall they are pulling triggers instead of squeezing them. "Now your breathing is important; take a deep breath in and exhale. Again, at the end of an exhale before you inhale, I want you to aim at your target and pull the trigger. You have your best control at the in between" Slowly, the girls began to fire a round down range, three of them hitting a target. "I want to do a couple more rounds."

"Very well done. ladies. They looked over their targets; each had at least marked them. Two had pretty good shot groups. Ok, looks like a couple of you might be pinching or pulling the trigger. Let us go back and put dimes back on." They went back, and she placed a dime on the top of each of the guns. She explained if the dime fell off then they were pinching the trigger and that would throw off their shot. If the dime stayed in place then they had a smooth trigger squeeze. After about twenty more rounds they all had were doing pretty well. Delaney had Reese show them the prone position and how to hold their weapons steady. Then his mom sent him down to the targets and put him on the rope. She then explained hitting a moving target. Reese pulled the rope to move the targets left and right while the girls tried shooting them. Delaney got down in the prone with each girl, learning their names, and helping them.

After the shooting lessons, all of them walked the playing field to learn how to use the terrain to their advantage. They learned pros and cons to the terrain. Reese demonstrated so the girls could burn it in their memories. Coming up on the shed, she explained how Reese and Jay worked together to eliminate players and survive themselves. The girls took it all in like little sponges. Delaney explained how the boys had buddied up to have each other's back. She taught them that it could be advantageous for the girls should do the same. Buddy up and cover two directions at once, protect each other. It is alright to be afraid of the guns but remember safety and don't be afraid to use them. She reminded them that they have skills.

Walking them back to the training tables, she thanked them all for letting her and Reese be a part of this and for having them there. "Let me hear that inner warrior."

"I am beautiful, I am strong, I am a badass."

"Next time you play, have each other's backs, use those skills you all have, and give those boys a run for their money. You are beautiful, you are strong, and you are some badasses."

Reese helped Mr. Gillis put away the guns and the face shields. He wanted the targets left up a while longer. Reese then headed to the truck with his mom and put their gear in the back. During the ride home, Reese noted where he screwed up out loud to his mom. Delaney had to inquire a little more as to what he was referring. "I didn't predict you would move." Delaney started to laugh. "Let me tell you how close you were to hitting me. If your aim had been a half inch higher, you would have hit me in the shoulder and chest. I almost didn't get out of the way in time." Both were laughing. "Always the bridesmaid, never the bride." The rest of the ride was just mother and son time.

CHAPTER 5

Delaney arrived her normal 15 minutes early, dressed in jeans and a nice sweater with a scarf around her neck. She was not real clear if they were going out to eat or if he was cooking. Once she entered the house, she could smell the Italian seasonings. God, she loved when the smell of food filled a house with richness and welcome. Ari had informed her dinner would be ready in a moment and to have a seat. He walked her to the table and pulled the chair back for her. The table had candles and wine, which was a romantic gesture. He asked her which salad dressing she preferred. Then he brought her salad topped with ranch and a basket of homemade bread. He then went back the kitchen and brought out a platter of spaghetti and meatballs before taking his seat next to hers.

"It's not fancy, but I don't know anyone who doesn't like spaghetti."

"Oh yes, my body, built by food, would die if I ever tried to skip the carbs." She giggled.

Ari just kind of looked at her because he could see nothing wrong with her body. He could tell she was fit and it was the first time he ever noticed her make a typical womanly body shaming comment. It had thrown him off guard for a moment.

"I see nothing wrong with your body," remembering the day she wiggled out of muddy clothes in his driveway and smiling at the thought.

"Don't get me wrong, I like my body with its flaws and all, but I like to eat too. More than I like to exercise."

Conversation was light during dinner. He noticed she barely touched the wine, and she only ate the lettuce, cheese, and croutons from her salad. Obviously not a fan of onions or tomatoes, mental note made. However, she ate a plate of the pasta and three slices of bread. They talked about how Reese was still gloating over his mama not getting him. How Jamison was in no hurry to play paintball again. She told him she had met with the JROTC girls on Saturday, to show them some stuff and to help them maximize their skills. She was kind of excited about that because she knows what a struggle women face still in the military and she wanted to give them a boost of confidence. Once dinner was done, she offered to help with dishes. He politely declined. He grabbed her a soda out of the fridge and took her by the hand to the patio. His backyard butted up against a flower garden before blending into a tree line. It was stunning and relaxing.

They sat there in silence for a few minutes. He watched as she took a drink of that pop and could not help but notice how her lips gripped the top of the bottle. How her hand held it with the pinky out like she was sipping tea with the queen. How beautiful she was as her lashes lowered and she breathed in the scenery and smells. He could not stop the thoughts beginning to race through his head. Her presence awakened something that had lied dormant in him for a long time, if it ever even surfaced before; it wasn't noteworthy.

"I don't find you intimidating, intriguing yes, intimidating no."

"That is because I have not let my freak fly, yet. Yet."

"You don't show your true self to just anyone, why?"

"Mention blindfolds and restraints and people have a tendency to get very uncomfortable. Bring up how you like to dominate a submissive and all they hear is *taboo*. Like how you just adjusted in the chair at the mention of it tells me you are curious but not that confortable with it. I imagine visuals of embarrassing moments or compromising positions came to mind, because most people who aren't familiar with it almost instinctively drift to the S&M of SMBD. It is easy to visualize pain, humiliation, and degrading behaviors; we see it every day in the world and on TV. That is such a small part and not the largest practice. All of it takes trust, communication, and a desire to please or be pleased. It is a heightened turn on that is not for everyone. Not everyone wants to be spanked, hair pulled, or restrained. With that being said, you would be surprised; more people think about it but never free themselves to try it than you might think."

"Damn, are you sure you can't read minds? Most men I know probably find it taboo."

"I find that hilarious."

"Please do explain."

"Did you know the only difference between being blindfolded and keeping your eyes shut is psychological. Your experiences and behavior dictate how it is perceived. Do you trust me enough to prove it?"

"Alright," *with only a slight hint of hesitation.*

She grabbed his hand and walked him back into the house because she figured as private as he was, outside and the excitement of getting caught might not make for his best first experience. She then put his hand on the counter as a grounding point. She set her pop down by his hand then moved in front of him. She looked him straight in the eyes and cracked a slight smile. It was a wicked gleam of amusement that shined in her eyes that made him swallow harder than he wanted to. She began to untie her scarf without ever breaking eye contact. She slid it slowly down one side of her neck. Arching one eyebrow, she flashed him the most innocent of smiles as she slid that scarf between both hands. He watched every move she made. Then she placed that scarf over both his eyes and tied it at the back of his head.

"You have this here, touching your hand, so you don't become disorientated. I promise I will not hurt you, nor will I leave you in any compromising positions. We can stop anytime you want or if it just feels like too much, just say the word."

He swore he could hear her smiling. Every nerve in his body was on high alert. When she ran her hand down his arm to his hand, every nerve tingled and fired excitement through his veins. Anticipation and nervousness were colliding just beneath his skin. Her voice was low and sultry as she touched his face and ran her finger over his lip then straight down to the first button of his shirt. Her hands moved swiftly through the buttons, having him lift his hand off the counter for just a second, and before long his shirt was gone, somewhere, he assumed the floor. He could hear her growl in approval right before she raked her nails lightly down his chest. His cock involuntarily jerked at her touch. *Heaven help me!* Her hands gripped his biceps and then her mouth placed soft kisses to his chest. It felt unreal. Everything so amplified. Her lips were warm and soft. When she tongued his nipple, a throaty moan escaped his lips that he had no chance of stopping. She sucked in a breath of cold air before she covered his nipple with her hot mouth again as she tightened her grip on his biceps. Then she lightly gripped his hardened nipple between her teeth before letting go and giving it a soft kiss. It was an erotic pain followed by softness. She then did the same to the opposite side, letting her tongue flick and twirl around the nipple.

"Oh how I like how your body reacts. Uninhibited and uncontrolled," she growled as she ran her finger down the length of his hard-on. He wanted to jump, but with no forewarning all he could do was absolutely enjoy her torture, or was it pleasure? Her torture was doing crazy things to him, and his mind was on overdrive. Hell, he had all he could do to make a coherent thought at this moment. His brain was spiraling out of control just like his body. She was playing with him and proving her point.

If only she knew how on the brink of out of control he was. He wanted to touch her so bad. She was driving him insane. He could hear her moving to his backside. Then he felt her tongue trail up his spine and then back down. His body shivered and his cock pulsed harder. She placed kisses at the base of his back while her hands unbuckled his belt to the front of him. Once she had it undone, she raked her nails up his sides sending goose bumps throughout his body. He could then hear her move once again, back to the front of him. He then felt his button on his pants let go, then heard the zipper dropping. She then grabbed ahold of his pants and worked them to the floor. She lifted his right leg, slid off his shoe, then the pant leg before moving to the left. Panic set in for a moment when he realized he was standing in front of her wearing nothing but his skivvies and a blindfold. All he could hear was some commotion, but he could not see her reaction. All panic disappeared when he felt her warm hands slide up his inner thighs. One hand slid up each leg heading right for the center. He noticed her breathing was a little harder and a little faster.

All of a sudden he could feel her warm breath being blown through the silk of his boxers straight onto the head of his cock. It felt incredible. Then she pressed her lips all along the outline of his cock through the fabric. She tortured and tormented him for what seemed like forever. He had been un-knowingly fisting his hand to fight the pleasure. At one point, he believes he stopped breathing all together. When she stopped he had no idea what was coming next. He wanted more, so much more.

Then she stood in front of him. He could feel her ass press against his cock. When she grabbed his hand and began moving it across her stomach he felt the softness of her skin. Unsure when she removed her clothes, his brain went into overdrive. He remembered her changing her clothes in his driveway. He opened his hand and let her warmth and the softness of her body carry him away. Then she worked his hand up to her breasts. He could feel a silky material of her bra and then what felt like lace. Her breast filled his hand and her breath hitched. Her hips rolled against his, and he could feel the desire to be even closer to her, inside her. She reached back and fisted his hair and held it tight pulling it in a way that just felt exciting.

He took his other hand off the counter and moved it toward her other breast. With one in each hand he began to knead them. He found her erect nipples and rolled them between his pointer fingers and thumbs. With her back pressed to his chest, he was giving as well as he received. Her head leaned against his shoulder, and she hissed out a yes, yes, yes. He could feel his balls clenching and his cock throb with each word she spoke. She worked his hand off her breast and down her stomach to between her legs. The silky feel of those panties had his fingers twitching with excitement. Then she parted her legs a bit more and slid his hand to her crotch. He slid a finger across that wetness as she let out that sexy little moan of hers. She was obviously tormenting herself along with him. He kissed her collarbone and neck while his fingers slid back and forth across her slit. His other hand gripped her breast and pulled her tighter to his chest. Yanking his hair, never letting her grip loosen, she ordered him to nip her neck at the same time he slipped his fingers in her.

"Maybe I should go and not wear out my welcome." She felt him grip her tighter. "Nah, I want you to see me, see what you do to me."

He took his right hand off her breast, keeping his left hand moving between her legs, and slid the blindfold upward. It took a second for his eyes to adjust. She was radiant, her skin reddened with want. Her breathing ragged. He kissed her neck and saw the clip to her bra in front. He pinched it and it popped right open. Her breasts never moved; they were as firm as he had felt. Now that he could see he kneaded the breast for a moment before focusing some attention on that little pencil eraser sized nipple that was begging to be caressed. She was wet, and he rubbed her clit with just enough pressure to make her gasp. She reached behind her and began to rub his cock through the silk boxers, with a merciless pressure. Then she slid her hand into his shorts and stroked his cock. His breathed hard against her back.

He pulled his hand off her chest and slid her bra straps off. God, she was beautiful. Her tanned skin felt so perfect under his hand. His desire just amplified once he uncovered his eyes. He could feel her, see her, and he wants more of her. He wanted all of her she would let him have. He desperately craved her, and that was reigning supreme. She brought out something in him that he had never experienced before. He can't put his finger on it at the moment, nor does he want to, but she changes him.

"I want you," she growled out.

God, she didn't have to say it twice, although he does still think she has some mind reading capabilities. He finds their thoughts are in sync just way too often to be coincidence. He used both his hands to slide her panties to the floor then his. There she was, naked, and wanting him as bad as he wanted her. It felt more like a dream than reality, maybe because the blindfold had messed with his senses a bit or maybe it was her and how she takes his brain to all new levels his body wants to devour. Option two was more likely the correct choice.

He spun her around, stepped to her, touched her beautiful face, and then kissed her with such a hunger and need it stole her breath. He used his other hand to pull her closer, feeling her breasts against his chest. The heat coming from between her thighs was calling his cock with the power of a siren's song. He could not take much more when he broke off that kiss, bent down, and swooped her up, carrying her down the hall to his bedroom. He didn't want his first time with her on the floor; that just didn't feel right.

He set her down on his bed and laid her out on her back. He looked at how sexy she was naked and wanting him. She looked like an angel with desire in her eyes.

"So wickedly beautiful with some kind of vexing power to drive me crazy."

He crawled in next to her. He ran his finger down her neck and then moved his mouth to her nipple. They were more than a mouthful but they fit perfect in his hands. Her nipple hardened under his tongue. His approving moan vibrated against it. When he sucked it in, her back arched putting her body closer to his. Oh the things he wanted to do to her. His hand started working its way down her body. He turned to watch as his hand slid down her upper thigh to her knee and back up again. Her legs opened a bit wider. He let his fingertip trail from her one thigh to another skipping over her sex spot. Then he trailed that fingertip back to the center and followed her treasure trail right to the spot. She gasped and let out a little moan; that sexy little moan is enough to push him to the edge and if he is not careful, right over it.

He ran his finger up and down the slick folds of her slit. She was soaked. Then he parted those folds and pushed the tip of his finger against her button. She fisted his comforter, ached, and leaned her head back. The sight was enticing. He tormented that button while moving his body lower and to between her legs. First he slid his finger to her entrance; then he put his tongue on her button and began his assault. He barely had the tip of his finger in when she moaned and clenched. Damn she was tight, and that clenching was making his cock rock hard and wanting.

Everything he was doing to her was sending her head spinning. Her pussy was aching for more. Sucking her clit was shooting sensations of pure pleasure throughout her body while his finger was beginning to build a pressure within her. His finger in her pussy felt so good, but it just wasn't enough. She wanted to feel his cock against that aching want, his body against hers, and she wanted to cum. She was wanting, and her body was demanding it. Her nerve endings were on fire with desire. Her body was begging to feel more of him and yet not enough. It was torture, and she is not always the most patient.

She finally grabbed his shoulders and motioned him up to her. He got to his knees and rested his cock right at her entrance. He entered slowly because she was so damn tight. She moaned as he got the head in. Then he watched as she bit her lower lip as he went a little deeper in. It was a slow going process because he didn't want to hurt her. She gripped his cock so tightly he had to focus his self-control.

It had been a long time since she had had sex, and her pussy was retaliating. Those muscles clenched around his head and refused to unclench. She might have felt embarrassed if the pleasure and want hadn't drowned that feeling. She adjusted her hips a bit to angle him slightly different. God, he felt good inside her. She wanted more; she wanted all of it. Her mind was reeling, until he was all the way in to the hilt. He leaned down and pulled back just a bit and then pushed into her. He did that three more times before she hooked her feet at his lower back. His moan was incredibly manly and very sexy.

With her legs wrapped around him, he could feel her vagina muscles gripping him tightly and massaging his cock with each stroke. In his head he was sounding like a Tourette sufferer. She felt so incredibly good he wanted to thrust and pound into her but knew he couldn't because his cock was already threatening to explode. When she started rocking her hips while he was held tightly in her grasp, he almost lost it, and he was not ready for that to happen. Every time he thrust forward her breasts jerked upward teasing him. He had to still for a second.

"You feel so damn good," he hissed.

She unhooked her feet and told him to roll. Putting his arm under her, he rolled to his back and she was now straddling him on top. He let his hands cup both her breasts and knead them. It was not long before both her nipples were hard with excitement and pointing forward. He rolled them between his pointer fingers and thumbs. She moaned and began to rock on his pelvic a bit wilder. She rocked forward and back, grinding her clit into his pelvic area. The sensation that caused was almost unbearable for him, adding a type of pressure to his cock that was new.

Before long she was moaning harder, and her nails bit into his pecks. He could feel her clench tight around his cock. Then her head titled back, and she almost screamed. She rocked back until he was buried to the hilt in her and then stilled doing only small circular motions. He could feel her muscles spasm around his cock as her release flooded his senses. Her fingernails bit hard into his pecks until she moved one to his nipple, tweaking it hard enough to bring a very pleasurable pain. He could feel the warm liquid flowing from her, coating his cock and trailing down to his balls, the searing pain to his nipples and her nails still biting his other peck became too much. That was when he felt the final warning sign jerk his cock. He grabbed ahold of her hips, digging his fingers in, and began to thrust upward furiously until he was groaning. The feeling of himself in her was intoxicating. Almost panting and gritting through his teeth, he thrust in deep and froze, feeling himself shatter inside her. Each spurt furious in its delivery. Her eyes were filled with such a storm of seduction that when he thought his orgasm was complete, his cock jerked one last time, leaving him depleted.

She leaned forward and rested against his chest. Her slight wheeze and heaved breathing took a few minutes to settle down. He stroked her back and moved her hair to the opposite side of his face. His cock was still resting in her. He was so elated and filled with energy at the moment, he felt like he could run a marathon.

God, she did not want to move from the position she was in. It felt good. She could hear his heartbeat in her ear and his hands caressing her back made her feel wanted. That was a feeling that both warmed her heart and terrified her. She had been alone for so long. She also didn't want to move because it was going to be messy. She could feel the liquid flowing. She turned her head up and kissed him.

"Sorry, I have to do it."

She pinched her vaginal muscles as she lifted off him but could not help some of the mess it made. She rolled off the bed and headed toward the bathroom closing the door. A few minutes later she came in with one of his washcloths, warm and wet, as she handed it to him. He cleaned himself for a moment, leaned up, kissed her, and told her he was going to shower. He even asked her if she would like to join him. Declining and beginning to search for her clothes, which were all still in the dining room, he was dreading her pending departure.

He showered as quickly as possible. He just had this horrible feeling that she had snuck out of his house without so much as a goodbye. Throwing on his pajama pants and heading down the hall, he was relieved to see her leaning against the counter, snacking another piece of bread.

"I hope you don't mind; for some odd reason, I am famished."

He couldn't help but smile; she made him laugh. Of course, she also made him crazy. Even now, he is watching her eat her bread, and a million thoughts are running through his head. He knows she has to leave and be home for her kid and yet he wants her to stay. He can picture curling up next to her all night and feeling her heat. Damn, she was sexy as hell without even trying. He finds that when this woman is around life just feels better. He wants her to know how much he enjoys her company, but he also doesn't want to make her run. Her friend Mazy told him he has to be careful, and after the first time she ran out after a great evening, leaving him no options of contact, he was not about to push her away. This woman tied his head in knots. The only thing he knows for sure at this moment is that he does not want this to be the end. He stepped to her.

"With everything in me I want you to stay; however, I know you have to get home to your son, and I respect that far more than my wants/" He wrapped his arms around her holding her tightly. "Besides, I could not promise you would get any actual sleep. You have awoken something in me that I never knew was there. "

"I know my life is complicated. Being a good mom is my number one job, and I would not trade that for all the money in the world. I have to make sure he grows up to be a good man. If it is any consolation, a big part of me wants to stay right here in your arms for as long as I can. It feels so nice. Then that just happened," pointing upstairs. "I could definitely handle more of that. I don't want to go, but I know I can't stay in good conscious. "

CHAPTER 6

*E*verything was driving her nuts today. She had the car to the mechanic about a month ago, who charged her a $140 to tell her he couldn't find anything wrong with it. Yet, every now and then she still feels that spongy feeling. Her boss was on her about cleaning up her case a bit, have it ready for a new sub. She lost her sub driver to a bigger, better paying route. She would never begrudge anyone that. With today being Tuesday, she has way too much time to think in the car. Things are just too perfect with Ari, even the sex. Weeks had turned into months with no idea how the time flew by. She has been contemplating how she feels about him for a couple weeks now. She is feeling those running shoes starting to call her name because to love someone again scares the crap out of her. She just needs to be done with her route today. She is thinking she might take her AK to the back forty to-night and blow through a box of shells just to clear her head.

Mazy has been riding her about how she was feeling about the man. It was starting to get on her nerves. How in the world could she tell Mazy how she felt when she wasn't sure how she felt herself. Mazy did remind her that dis-tance was not the answer. She knows Delaney better than most ever will. She knows when Delaney starts backing off and putting some distance that she is thinking about running.

After demolishing a couple of targets, she was feeling much better about the rest of her week until she got to work and her boss told her she was having trouble finding coverage for Saturday. Crap, that day she has a formal to attend with Ari. Oh how she hated the formal parties and fancy wear that she always felt uncomfortable in. *Crap, crap, crap.*

Saturday was here before she knew it. Mail volume was extremely heavy. The moment she loaded the car she was foreseeing a problem. She was starting to freak out about not having enough time to get ready. She called Mazy as she was leaving the parking lot. It was her mindset to cancel.

"The hell you are. I will meet you at your house and help you get ready. You most certainly will not stand that man up or cancel."

Delaney ran her route the fastest she has in a long time. She was running whenever she had to get out of the car. She got back to the office and ran her stuff in. She was not wasting any time. She called Mazy on her way home. Mazy, Nikki, and Cara were all waiting at her house enjoying glasses of wine while they waited. She jumped in the shower, and as soon as she donned her bra and panties the ladies got to work. One started blow drying her hair, another was in her closet picking a dress and shoes, and Nikki was pulling open a suitcase of make-up. Then the salon treatment from hell began. All Delaney could do was sit there. Nikki was a licensed cosmetologist and was working her magic with Delaney's make-up; Cara was putting her long hair in an up-do with Mazy's help. About an hour and a half later Delaney looked like a runway model. It was time to get dressed. She walked into her bedroom to see the dress Mazy picked was the royal purple satin dress with silver trimmings. She always liked that dress. It was funny Mazy picked that one. Once she was in the gown, the woman all wanted to give the seal of approval. Delaney walked out and strutted around and then twirled for the ladies.

"Oh hell no, sister. You better ditch those panty lines and grab you a t-back. How do you feel?"

"It definitely feels different without a 9mm strapped to my inner thigh."

"I'm sure you own some butt floss, although I don't think you could hide a gun there; maybe you leave the weapons at home tonight." *All the woman laughing in their wine induced giggles.*

"She probably wore that dress to one of those military shindigs with some high ranking muckety-muck in a foreign country strapped to protect his dignity or maybe hers, who knows. I get jealous sometimes when she talks about some of the stuff she has done. She probably did have a damn 9mm strapped to her damn thigh."

Goodness. First it's the fancy attire and shoes, then she has to break out the thong in order to not look tacky. She could just feel the tension building. Luckily it wasn't going to have time to build long; Ari was due in about 15 minutes to pick her up. She walked out and spun around. The ladies all approved and congratulated themselves on a job well done. Delaney grabbed Mazy's wine and downed it like a shot to settle her nerves.

"Perfume."

Delaney's house was pretty soundproof so she never heard Ari pull up. When she came back down the hall, he was standing there frozen in his tuxedo looking very dapper. She locked onto his eyes while she was trying to hook her bracelet and dropped it on the carpet. He walked over to her and picked it up and put it on for her.

"You look amazing," was all he could think to say. *Stupid, of course she looks amazing. No, she looks like a statuesque goddess gliding down the hall. She left you speechless and stupefied.*

They entered the kitchen to all three women with their cell phones out and ready like they were taking pictures of their children on prom night. Ari was a good sport about it and let the women have their moment. He thought it was a little odd that they were all there, but he learned long ago not to question the motives of women and never when they are gathered in the masses and you are the only man around; only a fool would step on that landmine.

"I am sure you can let yourselves out, ladies, and thank you for all your help. It means the world to me. Try not to drink all the wine," she said with a huge smile. "Don't wait up."

Ari opened the door for Delaney and waited until she was situated before closing it. Delaney and Ari got on their way to Great Falls. Conversation was light, and he could tell she was nervous. She was quieter than normal, plus she fidgeted her hands. He notices she does that if she is nervous or has a lot going on in her head. He figured it might be a little of both. He told her about how the dinner goes and how Jamison becomes a comedian at these dinners. She smiled knowing being in big crowds is difficult sometimes but knowing Ari and Jamison were there with her seemed to calm her nerves a bit.

Ari and Delaney pulled in about the same time as Jamison and his date Vanessa. A tall blond well versed in these kind of formal galas. She was dressed elegantly with small clutch in arm not draped in Jamison's. All Delaney could think was *this should be interesting.* The Velasco Hall was a beautiful Italian motif with Renaissance style. Classic rosette tiles, a few cherub statues scattered in the hall. Fine linens draped the tables and part of the walls. It really was breathtaking.

The four of them found their seats and began to mingle with the other guests. Ari introduced her to many people of all different backgrounds. She talked computers with one gentleman, engineering with another, accounting and payroll issues with another. Ari was surprised how well she conducted herself and held her own in conversation when she felt comfortable. He even opted to stand by and watch her work her magic. Some of those people had no idea what to think.

Then it was time to find seats again, listen to a small speech by Mr. Velasco himself. Delaney watched and intensely listened as he spoke. She could sense right away he was a fascinating man who came from nothing and worked his butt off to make his place in the world. She could hear the respect the man deserved and earned. She was only distracted for a moment when she heard Jamison whisper something about a gold-digging tramp on the arm of a new wallet. It caught her attention because she had never heard Jamison be so crude. Delany being as well trained as she is did not look around right away. She did however, in short scans, observe the crowd, until she could narrow down whom he was referring to.

It was safe to assume the woman he was referring to was none other than Aubrey. The infamous ex-wife. From the physical description Ari had put together when telling of his past and when she looks past the woman, she seems to be looking in Delaney and Ari's direction. Ari was not returning glances since he was busy talking to Jamison and another couple at the table during dinner along with myself.

After dinner, everyone was socializing. It was a very relaxed environment. One of the more enjoyable events Delaney could every remember attending. She could, however, feel a tension building that was not of her own. She had decided she needed a moment free from that feeling. She had excused herself from present company, found Ari, and told him she was going to use the ladies room. Ari kissed her on the cheek and told her he would wait there for her.

Delaney walked out the main doors and down a hall to a ladies room that was a little away from the main area. Quiet and a bit secluded. She entered the restroom to find herself alone. It was perfect for a moment to focus and deflect. She already sensed she was only going to have a moment. She breathed several deep breaths and mentally prepared for what was coming.

She was drying her hands when the restroom door opened and Aubrey came walking in. Delaney made a moment of eye contact, smiled, and then dug a lip gloss from her clutch. Applying the lip gloss slowly then rubbing her lips together to evenly apply while looking at herself in the mirror.

"Lovely party isn't it?" asked the woman also looking in the mirror sharing the space wiping at the corners of her mouth.

"Indeed it is," said Delaney.

The two exchanged smiles that lacked sincerity.

"I see you are here with Ari."

"Indeed I am," *while she gave her ringlets a little twist.*

Now Aubrey turns to face Delaney for the full intimidation tactic that it is. Look your enemy straight in the eyes. At this time Jamison had caught a glimpse of Aubrey look around the hall before heading out the main door and down a corridor that he swore he just seen Delaney walk down moments before. He was not having a good feeling about this. He dislikes Aubrey immensely and trusts her not. He scanned the crowd for Ari, and once he found him, he moved quickly to where he was. Jamison got his attention and whispered in his ear that he believes his ex-wife just chased Delaney to the restroom. Ari and Jamison excused themselves and headed in that direction. Jamison saw the look of fire in Ari's eyes that told him exactly how much he cares for Delaney. The two men stopped right outside of the ladies room but could not hear what was going on inside.

"Oh, *honey,* you are really setting yourself up for a huge disappointment," *with a tone of pure conceitment*

"Excuse me?" Delaney asked with a questioning tone.

"He will never come to love you. I was his first love, and I will remain his only love. He will never be completely over me. Therefore, honey, I am afraid you are going to be left disappointed."

At that moment Aubrey reached with her left hand to flip Delaney's curl.

Before Delaney could stop herself, she grabbed Aubrey's wrist in her right hand and spun it up to between Aubrey's shoulder blades while using her left hand to grip the back of Aubrey's hair slamming her face to the counter while stepping to the side for a more aggressive hold. The men heard something in the hall but could not make out what it was. There was no yelling like most catfights they had ever witnessed. They did not know if they should check or not. It would not be proper for men to barge into a ladies restroom. Delaney leaned over Aubrey's ear and began to speak.

"Aubrey, I am going to say this once and only once so pay real close attention. I am not the one you want to try to play these games with." Delany pulled that left arm up just a little higher to emphasize her point while her elbow kept pressure on Aubrey's face smooshed into the counter. "I will dislocate your shoulder in the blink of an eye and not feel a bit of remorse about it while I am trained to do by far worse." *Lie, she would feel remorse.* "What goes on between myself and Ari is our business and only ours. You ever come at me or try to touch me again, I will leave you barely breathing while I stand over your limp body and watch. Your soul makes my skin crawl in disgust. I am not intimidated by you nor will I ever be. If you feel you want to keep going down this road, game on, and I play to win." Delaney pulled that left wrist just a touch higher until Aubrey let out a strained painful sound. "I hope we understand each other."

Delaney let go of Aubrey then slowly grabbed her clutch off the counter waiting to see if Aubrey was about to make a huge mistake and cause her to become not so nice and not so friendly. Aubrey was still on the counter gathering her bearings as Delaney backed toward the door opening it slowly.

"By the way, *honey*, you are going to want to put some ice on that real soon and probably a heat pad later or you are going to feel it for a while."

Both men take a step back taking in the scene not real sure what to think. Delaney turns to see both men staring at her in disbelief. Once in the hall, her body surges with adrenaline and her hands begin to shake and fist. Ari starts to apologize for the situation that he had nothing to do with. Jamison is on cloud 9 saying she didn't see that coming.

"You know if thing with Ari doesn't work out, I am available. Damn woman, you just became off the charts in my book."

Ari looked at Jamison with a warning look in his eyes. Ari realized as the three of them walked back to main hall, Delaney needed to calm. He placed his hand on her back and leaned in to ask her if she would like a drink.

"Clear, cold, and non-alcoholic please. Thank you, and I am so very sorry."

Ari asked Jamison to stay with her while he got her something to drink. He had the bartender put some lemon-lime drink in a champagne flute. Meanwhile, Jamison is praising Delaney for putting the fear of God into that bitch. Remarking about the look on her face being one for his memory banks. How if he had been a woman he would have done that a long time ago, for his friend of course. Delaney barely registered any of what he was saying. Adrenaline still pounding in her ears and trying to purge the feeling of disgust from touching a woman like Aubrey.

Ari came back with her drink and handed it to her. He could see her hands were still shaking, and she looked like a combination of emotions: anger, disgust, apologetic, and many more. He didn't know where to begin to help her, but he has studied her enough to know he needs to. She is in public so firing down range is not an option at the moment. Ari put his hand at the base of her back and rubbed his thumb on the base over the silk of her dress. Her facial expression relaxed a bit. He then leaned in to speak softly in her ear.

"You have nothing to apologize for. You did nothing wrong. I am the one to apologize that you had to deal with my past. That was not fair to you in the least."

Delaney knew she should confess but right now at this moment was not the time or the place. She knows she must tell Ari the truth.

"We must talk to Mr. Velasco and then we can head out if you would like," Ari said to Delaney.

"I'm alright. There is something I must tell you when we are alone. I am looking forward to meeting Mr. Velasco. I found his speech to be inspiring. He seems to be a delightful man, good people to be around."

"Delaney, your intuition is spot on; he and my parents were good friends. I still go to his place and have dinner on occasion with him and the family. They are Old Country Italians all about heritage and history. Roberto said if I do not bring my lovely date over to meet him personally he will hand me over to Angelina. I don't even want to think about that," he said with a warm smile.

Ari, Delaney, Jamison, and Vanessa walked and socialized on their way over to where Roberto was chatting with a group whose back was to them. Three of them knew exactly who he was talking to and slowed in step. Avoiding the obvious for a long as possible.

"We can wait and try again in a bit."

About that time Roberto noticed Ari and the rest of his group.

"Ari, my boy, you and Delaney come, come," *waving hand forward and then to his right side.*

As Delaney was about to present her hand in a traditional handshake gesture, Roberto grabbed her hand and brought it to his mouth, kissing the back of it. Even Ari was taken by surprise for a moment but did not show it.

"Delaney, my dear, as gracious and beautiful as always. You make my boy shine like the stars in the night sky.

"You may not know some of the others. Trevor, CEO of Height Corporation, his date Aubrey. Roger, a retired engineer."

"We've met," as she looked at Aubrey and could see the telltale sign of slight fear and not moving fluently as before. A smile that would have been appropriate on a cat who just caught and ate the canary.

"And how do you know her, Roberto?" *Sounding like an investigation*

"For what this woman did for my granddaughter, I owe her the world. Her skills and character is magnifico and beyond reproach," *putting his fingertips to his mouth in an Italian gesture.* "Plus, she makes my Ari glow," *patting Ari's arm as he said it.* "She is an angel sent to tip the scales of balance back right in the world."

All knowing parties heard the huff Aubrey involuntarily let out with nobody really paying her no mind.

"Thank you, Mr. Velasco, for a splendid evening. I hope we will have future endeavors together. I am disappointed that we really must be going so soon," Trevor said.

"Do drive safe," Roberto replied. Delaney took note of handshake and tone was very cold and distant for an Italian who had just treated her like royalty. The wheels were spinning. While idle chatter hummed across the remaining group.

"Ari, my boy, please get Delaney another drink while I steal her away for a moment to Mama. Walk with me for a moment." It really didn't seem like a request as he took her arm and laced it in his.

"You have this crowd in quite the buzz. Some think you are Ari and Jamison's secret weapon; some are trying to figure out who you work for and can they steal you away. Some are just smitten by you in general."

"Not one for sure, and by that greeting you gave me, I am pretty secure in saying you are not a fan of hers. I was a little lost for a moment because I do not believe I know your granddaughter."

"Aubrey," *with a long drawn out sound*, "I threatened to disown my own son when he was seen out with her after the marriage between her and Ari ended. Best thing that could have happened to Ari. I knew his parents well," *giving the sign of the cross*, "wanting only the best for him. I spoke the truth; you helped my Abigail in ways her family could not."

"JROTC Abby?"

"Yes, my Abigail was very frustrated with the training exercises. She was tired of getting shot all the time. Mama wanted her to quit, but my Abigail is no quitter and has a strong fighting spirit. Myself, Christian Gillis, and her father tried to help her and Gillis's granddaughter but we lacked a woman's touch. Then you showed up at Gillis's place, and he knew right away you were the one they needed. A beautiful, strong, badass woman to help them find those inner warriors and build their confidence. Mama is not a fan of the chant but loves seeing Abigail succeed. Their last exercise, six of those girls survived using the tactics and skills you taught them; my Abigail and Amelia were two of them. I think they are feeling that chant in their cores. My wife wants to meet you and thank you personally."

"Abby was one of my favorites. You are right about her fighting spirit. She has an incredible inner strength. She just has to figure out how to tap into it on command. She will get there. I have faith that she will go as far in life as she chooses to."

"Mama, I present to you Delaney."

A dark-eyed woman took her hands and pulled them out to the sides and leaned in to kiss her cheeks.

"Lei e adorabile, non quello che mi apettavo." *She is lovely, not what I expected.*

"Grazie, penso?" *Thank you, I think?*

"You speak Italian." Both their facial expressions light up

"Molto poco." *Very little.*

The ladies smiled and chatted for a moment before Ari came up with another soda for Delaney. She was all smiles when his hand rested on her back. Roberto patted Ari's cheek and gave him a huge smile. Angelina was all smiles and told Ari he must bring Delany to dinner very soon. Not up for debate.

"I promise, Mama."

Ari and Delaney conversed with a few more people until deciding to head out. Delaney was kind of dreading the ride home because she knew she had to tell Ari the truth as ugly as it may be. They had found Jamison and Vanessa to inform them.

"I didn't realize you knew Roberto." Jamison directed toward Delaney.

"I had never met the man before this evening; apparently Abby benefitted from this badass woman assisting them."

"Oh yeah, let me tell you about Assassin Annie here on the ride home," Jamison says to Vanessa.

"Well, my brother, it is a lot longer ride home for us than it is you so we are going to get heading out."

They patted each other on the back and wished each other a safe ride home.

CHAPTER 7

*T*he four of them exited together and headed for their vehicles. Ari opened the door letting Delaney get in and get situated before closing it and heading to the driver's side. Once he was in, he started the car and headed back to Trave. It was about twenty minutes before Delaney spoke.

"I'm very sorry about the whole ladies room thing."

"What do you have to be sorry about? Aubrey is a cold-hearted, manipulative person. That is none of your doing."

"I'm sorry because I am to blame a bit."

"What are you talking about, Delaney?"

"After I heard Jamison say something, I assumed he was talking about her, because I could feel every ounce of it. It only took me a few minutes to figure out who and where she was. The vibe and all. After dinner I chose to use that restroom, isolated and away from the crowd. In the Army we call that a baited ambush." Then she took a deep breath and waited for the axe to fall.

"Go on; what were your intentions?"

"Well I went there with the intention of seeing if she would take bait. I was pretty sure she would. *I just didn't expect her to be stupid enough to be seen.* Then my only intention was to inform her that I don't like her type of games and I am not the type to be intimidated."

"Didn't look like just conversation from what I saw." She had trouble reading this statement because it was calm with no tone behind it.

"It started as conversation. I had no other intentions, I swear. Then she tried to touch me. That is when I instinctively put her in the hold position you saw. I didn't hurt her—well, not as much as I could have. She is going to feel that shoulder, and for that I do feel a little bad. I am trained to kill people, ya know. I reeled myself in quickly and did not lose my temper. I have to tell you she makes my skin crawl. She is not a good person at all; her soul is black and cold. I believe I did make my point. I really just wanted her to know that I don't like nor will I play her games. That is just not me. I am sorry that it happened today and at Roberto's place. I am not sorry I had words with her, yet."

"By yet I am assuming you relate that to me and not the situation."

"Yes."

Then the phone rang and Aubrey's name came up on the caller ID on the radio screen.

"Hello, what could you possibly want, Aubrey?" He sounded cold and harsh; Delaney could feel the panic and bile rising.

"What the hell, Ari? Who is she? Roberto singing her praises like she is some kind of super human to anyone willing to listen. She is not someone who fits in."

Isn't that the truth, Delaney thought.

"She's a goddamn psycho. I went to the bathroom, and she threatened to kill me because she is jealous that you still and will always love me. She is not of our caliber and never will be. I don't care how fancy you dress her up."

"Let me halt you right there. She is really none of your business. You and I are no longer together nor will we ever be together again. I no longer love you, and there is no chance of that ever being an option again. You made sure of that. Plus, you followed her to the ladies room to try to play your immature games with her. I have never known her to lie about anything, and she already told me about your encounter. I highly doubt she threatened to kill you, but I am guessing you found out she is more real than you could have predicted or anticipated. She is more of everything. I like her and am hoping your little stint tonight didn't ruin this. I have nothing further to discuss with you, Aubrey. If you have anything further, you can take it up with my lawyer."

Using his thumb, he disconnected the call. Staring out the windshield trying to dissipate the anger that was boiling inside him. He really wasn't mad at Delaney even after finding out she baited and ambushed his ex-wife. He knows she is very smart and she is who she is; besides, Aubrey was the one stupid enough to take the bait. He is mad that Aubrey pulled this crap, said that crazy stuff, and pushed Delaney to a darker part of herself. Now Delaney sits next to him, quiet and withdrawing into herself deep. Mad as hell because he doesn't know how to stop it, combat it, or bring her back to him ,and they were almost to his house where she would more than likely leave and go home.

"Can you play pool in this?" As he ran his finger down the silk covering her leg before grabbing her hand and squeezing it in his.

"I don't know, maybe, but do you really want to spend more time with me? I am honestly not best company at the moment and my behavior today has been less than stellar, borderline atrocious."

He knew in her head she was running the gamut of emotions. Praying she didn't just endure a situation that screams RUN. He could read it on her face and in her mannerisms. He studies her with great importance and high regards. She is different in many ways, but she is also a woman with a big heart and a painful past. He knows he has to stop her from going any deeper within herself and closing off emotionally. She has her technique down pretty well and knows she will be unreachable if she gets there, even to him. By all means possible, he will stop that from happening. She connects most during conversation, especially topics she likes, and she connects strongly when you bring out her sensuality.

"A pool game is exactly what we need right now."

She turned and looked at him. He could swear he saw the flick of a fire ignite within her eyes. *That's right, babe, come back to me. She can't help herself when it comes to playing pool. It's her comfort zone most times. It not only calms her but brings out her sensuality if you play right. She is vexing and complex for sure, but by God she makes life interesting, reminding me to later thank him in my prayers for Jamison's help uncovering the thing.*

Arriving to Ari's, he got out, opened her door, and held his hand out to assist her. She took his hand and held her clutch and dress in the other hand. They navigate the walkway and went into the house. Ari turned on the lights, never letting go of her hand. He guided them slowly down the stairs to the pool table.

"I'll rack while you take off your heels."

The first game brought her back one step at a time. She was becoming more herself the longer they played. Conversation and her demeanor started to get their normal glow. He knew she was all the way back when she threw in a couple of sexual innuendos, and he saw the flash of her thigh-high stockings. That silk clung to her body that left little to the imagination other than what it would look like pooled at her feet. She causes strange things to trigger in his brain, thoughts that would have never crossed his mind before. He didn't regret any of them.

"Can you play distracted?" he asked with a devious smile as she began racking the pool balls.

Before she could even answer, he stepped into her space and ran his hand down her right ass cheek. The silk felt smooth and warm. When she shivered and wiggled, he knew she was up for some play. Tonight, he was hoping to dissipate some of that angst he felt.

"Careful, you might be playing with fire."

"I sure as hell hope so; it got a bit chilly for a moment earlier."

Ari grabbed both of her hips, pulling her ass tight to his crotch and shimmied left to right. His cock was pulsating in anticipation. He heard her breath hitch, and all of a sudden he felt an overwhelming urge to dominate her. He slid one hand up her back to the base of her neck. He then grabbed her hair lightly and pulled her upright against his chest. She gasped in surprise. He took his left hand while holding her hair in his right and started to work the zipper on her dress downward. Using his left hand, he worked that dress all the way down until it pooled at her feet. There she was on display for him. Black bra, black silk thong, and black thigh-high stockings had his cock's full attention.

With her hair still gripped in his hand, he whispered in her ear while taking in her scent. "Dear God, Delaney you are so beautiful and so distracting. You make me think and want to do things I have never done before. I want to try new things with you. Like spank this perfect little ass for your bad behavior earlier and just to see what it feels like. I know you can feel how bad I want you. How bad my cock wants to feel the heat of your tight wet little pussy."

Damn, he may be new at this, but the man knows how to get my body humming. Aching with want.

"Yes, I was so bad earlier, and I definitely deserve a spanking or two," she practically growled out.

He released her hair and let his fingers trail down her bare back. As he did, she leaned down on the pool table and wiggled that ass ever so dauntingly.

His fingers found that black silk that parted her perfect ass. Each cheek fit perfect in his hands. He gripped those cheeks with pressure until they started to redden; then he went with what he was feeling. First he gave her right cheek a light smack. She gasped and leaned deeper onto the pool table. God, that just turned him on even more. He gave the second blow to that right cheek with a little more gusto. His hand tingled, and her cheek turned a beautiful shade of red. He rubbed it and kneaded it, feeling the heat in his palms. It was scary and extremely erotic. He shifted his position and smacked her left cheek with controlled pressure. The sound, feel, heat, and excitement of it all was a lot to process. His mind went into euphoria. No thought to what society believes is proper behavior, only him and her in this moment. He bent down and kissed her ribcage as he kneaded that hot ass. His kisses trailed down to those pink cheeks and kissed them softly before nibbling them. She arched, and her breathing became heavier. Then he slipped one finger between her legs to the sweet spot. He was pleasantly surprised at how hot and wet she was. How that silk felt heavenly under his fingers. She wanted him as much as he desired her.

This was exactly what she needed. Her mind stopped thinking and started only feeling. It was amazing. After her encounter with Aubrey, she wasn't even sure if Ari was going to want to see her anymore. She thought about it on the ride home; if that stunt she pulled had caused him to tell her goodbye, she would have been heartbroken and kicking herself. She was thanking God that he didn't do that on the ride home. Now, here they are, with his hands taking control of her body and sending her mind soaring. He just seemed to read her like a book, not skipping any of the footnotes. He felt like a dream come true, which doesn't happen to her ever—no wonder she is feeling so confused about what he really means to her. She knows she likes being with him; she didn't want it to end.

He stood back upright and unhooked her bra while rubbing his hand across her back down toward that thong that was tormenting him. He hooked his pointer fingers under that silk and slid it downward. It landed on top of her dress. He left those sexy stockings on. Damn she was beautiful. The word mine started singing in his head like a skipping record. It took him by storm because he knew she wasn't his yet. He doesn't really know how she feels about him. Right now he can't focus on anything but her and how she makes him feel. Tonight he feared losing her especially when she was quiet; he knew she was in her own head. But at present his animalistic side is what she needed, and he is going to give it his best shot.

He unbuckled the belt and undid his pants letting them fall to the floor. He leaned her back over the pool table a little more forcefully and rubbing his fingertips across her back harder causing a bite to her skin, she moaned but not in pain. Every part of her body felt as if kissed by the sun, warm and awake. He rubbed himself across her bare ass a few times before leaning down to whisper to her, "Your punishment has only begun, my dear. The things I am going to do to you are going to keep you thinking of me. You torment me with the extremely sexy ass that gets my cock hard with excitement. A whisper of a moan escapes that pretty little mouth of yours and it's a siren's song to my ears. Oh, I plan to punish you real good tonight, baby."

He trailed kisses down her ribcage, ran his tongue along her spine, before he clapped both hands on her ass cheeks while getting on his knees. He kissed both cheeks and then let his tongue wander up and down each of her inner thighs. She gasped loudly when his tongue licked right in the center sweet spot. He used both thumbs to spread her a bit farther while digging the rest of his fingers in to grip her ass cheeks and keep her from wiggling. Then he plunged his tongue in deep to taste the honey she was dripping with. Dear God, it was euphoric ecstasy. Tasted sweet and made him picture heaven. Her sexy moans were the songs of angels. This woman was nothing he expected or has ever encountered before. She was passionate, honest, a hurricane, and at this moment she is his.

She turned around, sunk down, and mounted him. She was so wet he slid in with ease. She put her hands on his shoulders and used her whole body to roll and rock herself across him. It was deep and stretched her to the max, but it felt exquisite. It was soft and intimate, intense but was perfect. Her breasts in his chest teasing him with an invite, he could not resist. Rolling those nipples between his taunt lips had her crying out. When she did, he grabbed ahold of her lower back and used his upper body strength to grind himself in to the hilt. She gasped and moan; then he felt her muscles tighten and spasm as she ground herself down on him hard. Then she leaned her head back and growled out his name as she shattered all over his cock. That was too much. He could feel his cock twitch at her pulsations and vise grip; he had no ability to hold it back any longer. He grabbed her hips and slammed in deep; a few thrusts like that and his seed was shooting hot streams of himself into her. She milked and massaged his cock for everything it had. Then she collapsed on his chest, heaving and breathing hard. He held her feeling her heartbeat strong on his chest. The smell of her hair from being damp with sweat permeating his every breath. Her skin is silky under his fingertips, and when she rolled her head to smile at him, he swears to God she glowed.

This went on until the early morning hours until they were both depleted and exhausted. He took her by the hand and walked her to his room. She did not put up a fight knowing Reese would not be home tonight. There was no way after that marathon she had the energy or desire to drive home. He gave her a tee shirt and pair of boxers. Even with her hair a mess and her face flushed, he couldn't help but think how beautiful she was. He pulled back the covers and let her decide which side of the bed she wanted. Once she was comfortable, he slid in behind her and held her tight. He was making mental notes of everything until he dozed off into a deep sleep. She was asleep about the time she hit the pillow.

She woke in the morning to unfamiliar surroundings. It took a second to gather her thoughts and her bearings. Waking up in Ari's arms felt amazing. It had been a lifetime since she felt that secure and wanted. It was causing an odd sensation to warm in her chest. To overnight with a man was a huge step for her, and to be held by him was an intimacy that scared her a bit. Then the reality came trudging in: She had nothing to wear home. She couldn't put on the dress and didn't really want to. Then she remembered she was wearing his tee shirt and boxers. Yep, he was going to have to loan them to her for a bit longer.

Getting up out of that bed was hard. She thought she was almost there, when he spoke and startled her. "Are you sneaking out?"

"No, I would never."

"Good, figured you might need some nourishment after last night."

After a good hearty breakfast of hotcakes and bacon, it came time that she had to get going home. It just felt so odd as she was contemplating it in her mind. Something about it just felt off to her. She felt as though a part of her was off kilter. He got real quiet after breakfast, and she was praying he did not regret last night. Lord knows she was having enough inner turmoil for the both of them.

He was regretting breakfast coming to an end. He knew she would be leaving soon, and that just was not anything he was looking forward too. He rather enjoyed her company and her conversation. He never thought of himself as lonely, but when she was around he just felt alive. She brings out things in him that he himself did not know existed.

Delaney knows she must get going. She needs a shower, clean clothes, and to get her head straight before Reese got home. He is like her and will sense this inner turmoil that she can't seem to shake. She feels like she doesn't want to leave but also knows she cannot stay. This doesn't happen to her. She has been on her own for so long; she is a rogue. This is a new experience for her; she misses him, and she hasn't even left yet. The drive home is going to be busy dissecting this new development.

That drive home felt like eternity, not thirty minutes. She could still taste his goodbye kiss on her lips. Her thoughts spiraling down the rabbit hole at mach speed bouncing off the walls. The "L" word even popped into her head once or twice. She was missing him before she even pulled out of his drive. She could smell him on her, taste his kiss, and recalled what it felt like in his arms. She is beginning to feel like that deer on a full sprint down the hill not noticing the bright headlights heading right for it until it is too late. The shower and clean clothes didn't even help her reel in those thoughts. She was frustrated and couldn't figure out why.

She went to the cabinet and grabbed the .45 and two boxes of ammo. Then she stomped her frustrated ass out to the range. After the 5th clip was unloaded, she felt at least back in control of herself. She had not heard Reese get dropped off. He had decided to walk up the driveway instead of pulling all the way back to the house. When he heard the distinct sound of the .45, he stopped at Nana and Papa's to see if they knew what was going on. He knew she had that formal with Ari last night, and today she is rapid firing the .45m; all he could think was this can't be good. Nana said she hadn't seen her this morning. Papa remarked how she didn't come home last night or she sat in the dark all night, but he never heard her car until a few hours ago. She's been out there shooting for a little over an hour. "I'll take some new targets out there tomorrow 'cause I guarantee she blew the shit out of those ones." Papa winked right before Nana got on him about the language. "Oh hell, he is a teenager, love. I promise it isn't his first rodeo around a little salty language."

Nana rolled her eyes and thought like father like daughter. Piss that girl off and she sounds more like a sailor than a lady.

Reese was about done cooking a box of mac 'n' cheese when his mom came in the back door. She looked exhausted and a bit mentally preoccupied.

"You want some?"

"No thanks," as she rounded the corner to grab the gun cleaning kit and plunk down at the table.

Reese finishes his mac 'n' cheese; filling a bowl to the top, he sat down by her watching his mother until he couldn't let her silence deafen him further.

"How was the gala?"

"It was good until I had a little run in with Ari's ex-wife. I baited and ambushed her. I almost lost Ari in the process of being me. Please let me be the first to remind you violence solves nothing, and I don't care how someone gets under your skin, don't ever let them get the best of you."

"Oh shit, did you kick her ass?"

"Boy, you better watch your mouth. I am not raising a heathen. But no, I did get real angry real fast, and I put her in check when she tried to touch me. Unfortunately, Ari and Jamison were standing outside the bathroom knowing potential trouble was occurring on the other side of that door. I don't believe she will ever try that again. I think I pretty much put the fear of God in her. I then had to wait to see if Ari was going to cut sling load on me. It was unnerving and my own fault. I had a selfish moment and did not use that lump three feet above my ass wisely."

"By the looks of the carbon on the clothes, you were out shooting for a while. Are you alright?"

"Yes, just a lot on my mind. I stayed the night at Ari's last night. Feel a little out of sorts today."

"Well I like him; he is pretty cool. I am glad you guys are alright. He is good for you, Mom. You know you got lots of love to give, and you probably could use a little more of it in your life." He grabbed his bowl and took it to the sink. Walked back to the table and kissed his mom on the top of her head reminding her to the moon and back before heading to his room.

She knew she couldn't hide from Reese; he is to smart and just like her at sensing when something is off.

———❧———

Ari was not faring any better. After a few hours of work, he found himself wandering around the house feeling lost. He was so thankful when Jamison called to take his mind off the fact that his house felt lonely and extremely quiet without Delaney's smile warming it. He can't remember a woman having this effect on him ever. He and Jamison talked about it and how strange it all was, kind of foreign. Jamison could tell by the conversation that Ari was falling in love. The mail lady has vexed him. She snuck in and flipped his world upside down, but Jamison knows Ari like a brother. She brings out the best in him and is nothing like that bitch he was married to. Delaney might be a reincarnated witch, but if she is, she is Glenda. Although the look on Aubrey's face comes to mind when the bathroom door swung open might make you think otherwise. Jamison remembers what she did to Ari's heart and figured with Delaney's God-given gift that she was not about to be played by a black soul if she even has one. In secret he wished Delaney would have knocked that shit out of that bitch, but Delaney is a lady under that pistol-wielding, hard exterior of hers, and his best friend is head over heels about her. He is also scared to tell her because of her tendency to run. Damn women anyhow.

CHAPTER 8

*D*elaney and Mazy were having lunch and catching up; it had been a while. They were eating and chatting about what was going on. The subject of Ari came up. Listening to Delaney go on about how good things are, Mazy started to read between the lines. Her friend was saying how beautiful things were going, and her body language was revealing Delaney at her running stage.

"You think because things are close to perfect for you that the walls are going to come crashing in. Why do you think you don't deserve to be happy? He makes you happy and treats you well. You always tell me you are hard to love because of what you are. Here is a guy that does not cause your spider senses to tingle, is completely honest with you so far, and even plays your kinky damn games, and you want to run because it feels perfect to you. You so piss me off; my marriage is shit, and I would not know how to act if a man like Ari was interested in me. What the hell is wrong with you?"

"I don't know. If I knew I would fix it. I would not be afraid of this feeling. I wouldn't feel this overwhelming urge to tuck tail and run sometimes. I didn't feel this way about my husband. When he died I wasn't sure I ever truly loved him. I questioned myself and the outcome was not favorable. Not like my unconditional love for Reese. It feels too good to be true. He is dependable and sweet, authentic, trustworthy, exciting, and he is open-minded, playing my kinky damn games as you called them. He stands up to me when he disagrees with something I have said or done, which means he is being completely honest with himself and me. He knows who he is but is not so set in his character that he doesn't grow and try new things. He is no people pleaser, but he damn sure pays full attention to actions. This feels unlike anything I have ever experienced. I'm not delusional and thinking he or myself are perfect. I am well aware we each have our flaws. These months don't seem like months; it seems like I have known him forever. Hours tick by in person or on the phone and it feels like minutes.

"OMG, not to give you TMI for a moment, but whether it is those kinky damn sex games or it is as vanilla as possible and feels like making love as I see it, I have never felt a connection with someone like that. There has been a few times it felt like the whole world was only him and me, like my consciousness left my body in a state of euphoria for a second. Half the stuff is unexplainable even to my rational and realistic brain."

"Wait a minute, hold the phone," *Mazy recalculating Delaney's words.* "You love him. I mean you really love him, like soul mate love him, and that is what is scaring the shit out of you. You feel vulnerable and could possibly get hurt which goes against your nature."

She leaned back in her chair and letting out a long breath.

"I take it you have not told him yet?"

"No, what am I going to say? You make me feel like this is all too good to be true and that gives me some crazy urge to run for the hills and push you as far away as possible because for some odd reason it scares the hell out of me. I can't talk to Mama because we took them to the airport the other day for their three-week vacation in Hawaii. She asked me what was wrong the other night. I told her a lot on my mind from work. Reese was grilling me when I was out shooting the .45 for an hour last night. My head is spinning out of control. I don't know what to do."

"You are going to put those big girls panties on, take a breath, and tell him how you feel. Sometimes yes, you pull them up so hard the elastic snaps and you show your ass a bit, but I think he will understand and he will probably surprise you. He went through hell and high water just to get a date with you; he and his friend if we are being completely honest. Besides, he may even feel the same way; you have no idea. Your gift won't allow you to see or sense matters of the heart."

"Is that totally true, or do I block them out as a self-preservation mechanism? I got some hidden talents, ya know."

"Oh I know all about your hidden talents. I have been your friend for a long time. You have been feeling an unexplained connection for a reason and for a while. You can only deny it so long, and I know you well enough to know that if you do not express yourself and your feelings soon you are going to explode. Did blowing shit up help? Hmm, I am going to say no confidently. That inner turmoil and unrest is not going to settle itself until you face it head on and confess your feelings towards him to him."

"I don't know. What if that is not what I am feeling? What if I am so wrong I ruin it? Or what if he feels that same way, then what? We live happily ever after in a white picket, fenced-in yard with cats and dogs curled up on the couch with us. I can't get a feel as to what can happen. I don't want to take that chance yet.

"Okay, I get what you are saying and I understand why you are afraid. You have been on your own so damn long that the concept of sharing your life has to feel about as foreign as being in a new country at first, but just like when you went to all those other countries, you changed and adapted to the new. Think of him as a new foreign country. You are there for a reason; navigating the new and unknown is different but not undoable. The worse thing that could happen is you tell him how you feel and he exits. I do not see that happening because he seems to be a very smart man, level-headed, and has survived the hurricane known as Delaney unscathed. Hopefully unscathed, you have never told me about cruelty and hatred style S & M. Oh, you are a freak but not in a bad way, and your style is a bit intimidating, but I still love ya. I never know what is going to come out of your mouth or festering in your brain when we see a simple item like a leather leash."

Both ladies are laughing and finishing up their lunch. Delaney has an evening with Ari tonight that she is looking forward to and not all at the same time. She hates the fact that she overthinks everything and becomes a self-mutilating ninja when she is beating herself up over feelings. She needs to make sure she truly does love him before she lets that cat out of the bag.

Delaney's drive home was filled with thoughts that were typical of her—all over the place. She had to giggle out loud when she thought about how close Reese and Ari had become and often tsk over who gets what leftovers are in her fridge or a bag of munchies in the cabinet and how him and Reese have in-depth conversations about physics and problem solving. Then she thought of all the ways he might react if she told him how she felt and shivered like a chill touched her bones. Mazy was right and knows her pretty well, enough to know she can't keep it secret much longer because it is eating her up from the inside.

Ari's phone: *She has a lot on her mind. She is quiet and distant. You need to help her get over the emotional hill she is climbing. Good luck and I will pray for you.*

Ari looked over at Jamison and shook his head. "These two really need to come with a manual and decoder ring."

Jamison started laughing, figuring he was referring to Delaney and Crazy Mazy, which is a nickname he came up with a while back. He couldn't help but ask so Ari showed him the text. Jamison read it and then reread it.

"What, you don't speak mail lady yet?"

They both chucked, and Ari began to gather up his files and reports knowing he had to finish up and get on the road. He was seeing Delaney tonight and not real sure what kind of situation he was walking into. If he remembered right, Reese had practice and was going to Jay's after. It would be just him and Delaney for the evening. He tried to figure out what Mazy meant by her text with no success. He decided he really did need a decoder ring.

Mazy was right; Delaney was a bit quiet and detached. Not so much distant, but he could tell something was just a bit off. He tried to approach her about it but damn if the woman was not the queen of sidestep. She avoided whatever was bothering her like the plague. He decided to use the bathroom; when finished, he turned to wash his hands, and something black and shiny caught his attention on the back of the bathroom door. Damn, it is a riding crop. A long, black, thin shiny, riding crop with a smooth leather swatch on the end with no horses in sight. A million thoughts went racing through his mind at mach speed. Then Mazy's text came into his mind, and then the craziest thought came to his mind. He grabbed the crop and headed back toward the living room.

"Am I safe to assume you do not use this on horses?"

She turned a pretty little shade of pink at the question.

"No, I do not use that on horses; it is actually brand new, and I have not used it yet, but in all honesty I bought it with you in mind."

Before he could stop himself and think about what he was saying, "Show me" came spewing out of his mouth, and his stomach instantly tightened with nerves.

"Are you sure, 100% sure? If you have doubts, this is not a deal breaker and I have no problem adapting."

"Yes, I am sure." Meanwhile, his nerves were screaming, *Have you lost your mind? She is going to domme us and we aren't equipped for that.* Fear and nervousness flooded his system; she could see it on his face and hear it in his voice.

She stared at him in disbelief for a moment, making sure he completely comprehended the magnitude of what he just offered. She gave him one last chance to retract before the opportunity was just what she needed and too tempting to pass up. She was thinking a plan super quick in her mind that would not make him regret his offer.

"Well then, I shall not keep you waiting long. You have 15 minutes to remove your clothing and sit with that riding crop. You will become familiar with that tool. I want you to feel the softness of the leather, smell it, swing it through the air to hear it sing, then snap it across your hand so your body is not caught off guard. Also you need to come up with a safe word, not anything like stop, something odd that will stop activity if it feels entirely too much or uncomfortable."

She rested her hand on his stomach and kissed his cheek before exiting toward her bedroom. She knew he was nervous and unsure. She also knew it was new to him. She had to come up with a plan that would not scare him and yet open his eyes to some new experiences, some very new experiences as she chuckled to herself. Her plan was to look intimidating but to take it easy on him, hoping his safe word never crosses his mind. She grabbed a black and red racy corset, a black thong, and dug her black shiny, thigh-high boots with heels out of the closet. Then she got in the last drawer of the closet and grabbed a collar, handcuffs, and the ankle shackles. She decided to put the shackles back, reminding herself to take it easy on him.

It took about twenty minutes to get herself clothed, hair thrown up in a messy bun, a dab of her favorite perfume to remind herself to feel sexy and keep it soft. Her black eyeliner making her eyes look wicked. She slid the collar in the back of her corset, wrapped the leash around her wrist, and held the cuffs in her hand. She took a deep breath and headed down the hall. She was so hoping he hadn't gotten so scared that he left. She was thrilled when she found him looking very nervous sitting on the couch naked with that riding crop draped across his legs.

Lord have mercy, repeated in his head. She looked like a devious goddess sashaying down the hall in shiny boots showing just how long and trim her legs are; then he noticed how she was spilling out of the top ruffles of that corset. Then his brain tuned in on the sound of the chains and the shiny item she was dangling from her hand. Every nerve in his body jolted to attention. Handcuffs! Thick shiny handcuffs like he had never seen before. Self-awareness kicked in. The look in her eyes was calm, until she stopped in front of him. She lowered her eyes, put her finger under his chin, and ordered him to stand. Right about now his body was yelling *run, run as fast as you can*, but nothing would move.

"Safe word?"

"Courage."

Oh the look in her eyes screamed she was about to devour him. She raised one eyebrow and let out tsk, tsk, tsk sound. She took that riding crop from his hand and dropped it to the floor then motioned for him to hold out his hands out with wrists up. That steel was cold as it touched his skin, and she took her time locking him up. She asked him if he was still alright. He had lost his ability to speak; all he could do was nod. His nerves wanted to scream *courage, please courage, just say it*. His brain and the adventure of where this is going would not let the word form in his mouth. With enough engineering experience, he knew by the keyed lock there was no getting out of these cuffs until she let him out. They were not painfully tight, but they restricted his movement completely. Then he noticed that look in her eyes; it was powerful and hypnotic. That was when she grabbed the chain links between his wrists and pulled him to the floor.

"On your knees"

It was clearly an order. He did as he was told. Once he was on his knees, she touched his face gently. Then she kicked her feet apart, and he could feel her power and dominance command his attention. She reached to her lower back and pulled out another shiny item. It dawned on him where she planned to put that larger ring with yet another key. She placed that cold steel collar around his neck and locked it in place. Then she took those three keys attached to a ring and slid it down her middle finger. The rattle they made was distinct. Then she leaned down and whispered in his hear in a sultry purr, "Since you still haven't said the safe word I am going to show you what it means to be my submissive."

His cock twitched at her warm breath and sexy growl: cuffed, collared, and on his knees. His body had never felt more alive and alert. Nervousness was still there but so was excitement. He was not real sure which one was strongest nor did he care at the moment. It was nothing new to have this woman have him a tangled mess. Then she flipped some ring on the front of his collar, taking her hand from there to her wrist where she began to unwrap what looked like a leather leash. She snapped that hook to the front of that collar, slowly sliding her hand down the length before clasping the end and pulling it towards her. Surprise was written on his face until she used her other hand to grab his hair and pull his head back.

"How this works is I give the orders. If you do not reply to my request or not in the way I want you to, I will punish you; do you understand? Only reply I want to hear is 'Yes, Mistress.'"

All he could do was look at her in shock. She was wild, but he had never seen this side of her. She let go of his hair and the leash. The leash hit his chest and dangled. He also heard those keys jingle. She stepped back and off to the side. She then crouched with her knees together and grabbed the riding crop. "That is your freebie. Look at me, and you better find your voice." She pulled that riding crop to an upright position while she spread her knees apart. "You will reply, using your voice, 'Yes, Mistress' or you will become very familiar with this," as she rocked the crop back and forth between her legs.

He had to clear his throat to reply, "Yes, Mistress." As the words rolled off his tongue, he could feel tension and excitement start to grow in every inch of his body. His eyes traced those black boots to her taut thighs and past to the sweet spot that that was clearly visible with her legs split like that. Covered by a little piece of black silk that he wanted to reach out and touch. She watched as his eyes wandered.

She moaned as she stood erect. She stepped behind him and leaned into his ear. "You like what you see and you want to please your Mistress, don't you?'

"Oh yes, Mistress."

She held the riding crop in her hand and used it to trace every inch of his body. She knew he was nervous and may need a little coaxing. This was new to him. She never introduced pain into the scenario, just erotica, and by the way his body was reacting, he got over his nervousness and moved straight to excitement. His body shivered and flinched at the touch of that riding crop. She figured out just how sensitive his nipples were and new ways to open his mind.

By the time she uncuffed his hands and grabbed ahold of that leash jerking his collar to just where she wanted him, he was ready to please her anyway she would let him. She used that leash to guide him on top of her, wrapping her heels around this lower back and locking them together keeping the points away from his skin. Still holding it tightly, she pulled him downward for a deep an intimate kiss as he entered her. Her wetness was matched with his rock hardness. It was something he never saw coming; never in a million years did he ever think he would find it so satisfying. She really opened doors to his body and soul with her softness and tenderness while completely dominating him in every sense. She made him completely forget his fear of the unknown. Sometimes there is no explanation; it's lines blurred of give and take.

CHAPTER 9

She woke a little earlier than her alarm thanks to the same nightmare that she still can't decipher. It was not an easy one to figure out what it meant, and she keeps waking up at the same place every time she has it. Trees moving at slow motion like a movie.

Reese came into the kitchen while she was looking out the window.

"Did you have that nightmare again?'

"Yes, just wish I knew what it meant. A sign of something to come, or does that place mean something that I should know? It just frustrates me because I can't figure it out. Is everything alright with you?"

"Sure. Life is good. Like everything else, Mom, it will be deciphered when it is supposed to be. Maybe it is one of those weird dreams that doesn't mean anything or has nothing to do with what you are seeing."

"Good point, this morning it just has me feeling a little off kilter. Just has me feeling like something is just not quite right, unbalanced or off somehow. Well, I can't dwell on it. I have to get ready for work, and you need to get ready for school. I see it's raining out so it is going to be a fun day of delivering. Nothing like a cold fall drizzle to add to the chill I am already feeling."

Delaney got the mail and packages loaded into the car nicely; today was a lighter day. She could see out the windows and had some room to spare. She took off to start the route; her stomach still wasn't feeling right, which happens sometimes when her spider senses are trying to tell her something. It wasn't going away. Reese was fine, time to call Mazy. After the ladies spoke, Mazy ran down her schedule with Delaney and nothing stood out. Mazy knew about the nightmares but had no real answers for her. Once she got done with her conversation with Mazy, she would give Ari a call. Her mom and dad were in Hawaii since Tuesday. Thinking about them had not made it tingle more so she ruled them out as well. She really was hoping she was just being paranoid and it would be fine,

She had to be very careful when she called Ari because she did not want to worry him for no reason. He knows what she is, but he has never seen her spider senses in action, and she did not want him to start thinking her some kind of freak. Plus for a couple weeks now she has been acting strangely around him because she has been trying to tell him how she feels about him, but fear is holding her back. He has already been asking her what is going on and is anything wrong. She is 99 percent they are her feelings and not what she is feeling come off him.

She felt no better when she got off the phone with Ari; he was working from home today and was looking forward to her stopping by to deliver the mail so nothing about his day warranted he stomach feeling like that. She decided that was enough time spent on trying to figure out what it meant and she needed to get her butt moving so maybe she could hang out at Ari's a couple minutes extra.

She was pulling off a cluster of boxes when she heard a strange noise in the front of her car; then she looked out the window and saw the trees moving in slow motion with a very immediate familiarity. She was about to enter a two-track with a 90 degree turn that already is not a favorite of her route. Today was rainy and cold so it added to uneasy feeling. She went to turn the wheel to the left to enter the two-track, but the car stayed going to the right. She took her foot off the gas, but she knew it was already too late. Like a slow motion film she was headed straight for a tree; she knew exactly why she kept waking up in the same place in her dream—the tree. "Oh shit, this is going to hurt."

Her car hit the tree, and she flung forward from the abrupt stop. Her head smashed into the rearview mirror, which is when she closed her eyes; then she was blown back by the airbags that went off. Oh damn it, her body felt like she just stepped in front of a semi. He ears were ringing in some high pitch noise that created a buzz feeling in her head, and she couldn't move. She could smell the smoke filling her lungs even though she had not opened her eyes yet. Her skin felt like it was on fire along with her lungs. One of her customers who had been in his garage had heard the ruckus, which was a good thing because this time of year the seasonals leave for the winter months so it could have been hours before anyone had found her. On a rural route like hers, you may not ever pass another car or few and far between. He was running to the cause of the noise while dialing 9-1-1. Once he reached her car, he was describing what he was seeing inside to the dispatcher

The car had steam and smoke rolling over the front of it; he recognized it as the mail lady's. It was making a hissing sound, but it was not running. He ran to the driver's side to find airbags that had not deflated enough yet to get a clear view of person inside plus the car was filled with smoke. He opened the driver's door, and smoke stinking of sulfur started pouring out. He pushed on the airbag deployed from the steering wheel to view her better. He saw blood. Using his calmest voice he told her help was on the way. He swore she said she was on fire; he barely heard her. He told her to try to stay still.

Stay still was not really an option. She ached everywhere and she could not breathe. She also didn't hear a word he said over the ringing in her head. Her eyes were open, but between the smoke and blurred vision, she could only make out a shadow moving. She could feel the burn in her chest and knew her asthma was becoming a problem; however, she could not get to her purse to find the inhaler. She could not find her voice and knew she was slipping. Hopefully help was coming and would get there soon.

Ari was on the phone with Jamison when the first emergency vehicle went screaming by his house. He looked at his watch, not really sure why, but when he did, a sinking feeling washed over him. Delaney should have been there by now. He told Jamison about the bad feeling he just had and how he was going to let him go to see if Delaney was alright. Once he got off the phone, he grabbed his keys and was already thinking about what direction her route goes backwards from his place. He was pulling out of his driveway just as an ambulance went by with the sirens blaring. He turned out behind it and followed it the exact way her route would go. The more he followed it the more his stomach started to tighten. When the ambulance slowed down past the two dirt roads he turned on, he still wasn't feeling all that relieved. He started heading toward the two-track she talks about often, and with it raining it would be even less fun. Once he rounded the bend, he saw the fire truck with the lights flashing. His heart stopped the moment he saw the white car smashed against the tree. He barely had the car parked when he was rounding the back of the fire truck.

"Delaney."

Panic setting in as the Ambulance rushed in between them and the Fire truck.

He watched as the EMTs took her from the car and put her on the gurney. Her body looked limp, and her face and hair were coated in blood. Her face was also red like it had been way to close to heat. He held her hand for a moment trying to stay out of the EMTs way. She never looked at him, but she acted as if she knew he was there. Her eyes were a dull grey looking like storm clouds, not the energy he was used to seeing in them. She was not focusing.

"I want to tell you I l-l-l…" Then her eyes rolled back, and she lost consciousness. The EMTs rushed her into the ambulance asking Ari her name and if he was her husband before whisking her off. All he could think was to say her name and let them know she had asthma. He watched as the ambulance with its lights blaring headed out of the two-track. A fireman handed him her purse minus her wallet, which they sent with her.

He stood there for a moment trying to gather his thoughts. Then he dug in her purse for her cell phone, scrolling through her contacts until he found her office number. Shelby started to about cry when Ari explained Delaney's accident and how she had been taken to the hospital. Russell had come to the office after hearing it on his walkie-talkie. He was hoping it wasn't Delaney, but when the ambulance relayed message to the hospital he knew the description. He told Shelby he was heading to the site and would let her know. Shelby told Ari that she would call the boss and let her know what was going on. Russell said he would grab the mail and finish the route.

Russell arrived just as the tow truck was arriving to take the car. He looked at the windshield and winced. There was a two-foot long chunk of hair blowing in the wind. The windshield also had a rip that was separated about a two-inch gap. There was also a perfect forehead print of shattered glass. The passenger door was hard to open; the fender was bent due to the impact, but he knew by the contents inside her contact was not fast or hard. The tow truck driver started to hoist the car after it was unloaded. The front passenger tire was not turning; it was just sliding in the mud. Broken tie rod, the tow truck driver remarked.

Ari was still there. He was looking a bit lost. Russell walked over to him and started talking. He told Ari they were taking her to the hospital, did he know how to get in touch with her parents. Ari informed him they were in Hawaii on vacation. Then he thought about Reese. He was holding Delaney's cell phone so he knew they would not be using it trying to get ahold of anyone off it. Ari looked at his watch and started coming up with some kind of plan. Since Russell had everything loaded, he made sure Ari was alright and took off. Russell didn't know that much about Delaney's personal life, but he did know she was close to her parents and her kid. The rest was a mystery; then he thought about the flowers that came to the office months back. He thought Ari looked like a flower giving kind. Delaney had been real quiet the last couple days.

CHAPTER 10

I *find myself surrounded by darkness. I can hear them talking about my* *stats and vitals in bits and pieces, but it sounds like whispers. I feel nothing,* *numb. My head is no longer ringing. It almost feels like a dream except* *I know I am not asleep. I am in a familiar place; I am deep within myself. I am not* *feeling pain, heat, or anything. I haven't done this in years, haven't felt any need* *to; how I developed the skill was a story I put away forever. The only reason I can* *think I am here is I am close to death or I severely panicked and sought safety in* *complete avoidance.*

I remember hitting my head into the rearview mirror. I somewhat heard people talking *around me, and my skin felt on fire. Oh, I remember feeling my chest closing off. I don't* *think I am dead, not that I would know what it felt like, but I do not sense being dead. I know* *I could sense Ari or I was projecting myself to him. I felt his warmth and his calming energy.* *Note to self: I really need to tell him how I feel about him. He deserves the truth. I just hope* *he can handle my complete honesty. I am afraid. With that my thoughts and I disappear.*

Ari was sitting at the end of the driveway waiting for the bus to drop Reese off. He had no idea what his schedule was today, and he was not sure what he was going to say to him about his mother being in a car accident because the hospital would not give him any information because he was not her spouse or immediate family, and the last thing he wanted to do was make matters worse. He would sit here until Reese got home; she would not want him to go through it alone. About 4:15 the bus came to a stop, and Reese stepped off and waved bye. He walked over to Ari's truck and could feel the tension instantly.

"What happened?" He just jumped right to the heart of the matter while getting into the passenger side.

Ari took a deep breath. "Your mother got in a car accident today. They took her away in an ambulance. I am not sure about her status because they will not tell me. The last word I got was they took her to Reed Hospital."

"She knew. She was talking about it this morning; she said something felt off kilter, and it was bothering her. She asked me in her subtle way fishing to see if it was me. I will bet she called you as well this morning fishing. I will also bet Mazy got a call this morning too. I know my mother. Her so-called spider senses were going off like alarms."

Ari stopped and thought about his conversation with her this morning. She just made idle chat about his plans for the day and not much of importance. She never said a single word about any gut feelings.

Reese took out his cell phone and found the number for Reed Hospital. He called the administrative number to find out what was going on with his mother. Good thing his mother taught him: her date of birth and some other vital information so they would tell him what was happening. He found out they transferred her to Great Falls, the Intensive Care Unit. Reese paled a bit while Ari stiffened in the seat. Both thinking the same thing: If she was transferred and in a specialty unit, it was not a good thing.

"Can you take me to Mom?"

Ari threw the truck into drive, and they were off. He already knew where the hospital was in Great Falls. Last time he was there, he said his forever goodbye to his mother. He prayed that this was not going to be that situation for Reese. He looked over at Reese and tried to be strong for him. He knew in his heart it was going to be a long ride and a worrisome one as well.

Reese broke the silence in a big way.

"Do you love my mom?"

Ari was taken by such a forward question especially after being alone with his thoughts that ranged from worst-case scenario to prayers. He looked at Reese and had to think how to answer that question. He knew what to say, he just had not said it to anyone out loud. Plus, he hadn't told Delaney yet.

"Well, young man, I have not told her how I feel about her yet. As you know, she is a bit skittish when it comes to that word and feelings in general, but yes I do love her. Man, that is the first time I said it out loud. It feels good to say it. Your mom has been acting a bit strange, and I haven't had the courage to bring it up."

Reese cracked a smile. "Yeah, isn't that the truth. I can tell you why she has been acting weird, or at least I have a really good idea. I believe she has feelings for you, strong ones. When she came in from shooting the .45 the other night, her expression wasn't hiding it well at all. I know my mom, and she is afraid. There are only a handful of reasons she would have fear because as you know my mom is a badass. She doesn't fear much, and she isn't afraid to tackle much. She has pretty much been mom and the dad role for as long as I can remember. I don't remember my dad, hardly at all. Normally, she steers clear of men, finds reasons that they have no potential in her life or mine and she dumps them. You are different; you know what she is and she hasn't reached for those running shoes Mazy is always busting her about."

Like her ears were ringing or something, Delaney's ringtone went off, and Reese grabbed the phone to see Mazy's name pop up. "Hello, Mazy."

Ari sat there listening to Reese tell Mazy about the accident and how they took Delaney to Great Falls in the ICU. He had to explain how he didn't know much more at the time, but he would update her as soon as he found out more. She reminded him that his mom was strong and entirely too feisty to be down and out for too long. She also reminded him that she is the most stubborn and thick-headed person she has ever had the pleasure of knowing; there was no way she wasn't going to fight the good fight. She also told him she would be on her way as soon as she could.

—◦—

Delaney found herself back in basic training in the middle of the live fire exercise. The smell of the gas invading her nostrils. It was dark and so loud. She could feel her heart racing as she was low-crawling under the barbed wire, bullets swishing overhead. She scraped her arm across one of the barbs, ripping her uniform and slicing into her bicep even though this time she did not feel it. The fear was so real, and she was reliving it as if she was there for the first time. She could not understand why she would be here again. She could do nothing to alter her reactions even though it was a nightmare. Her reactions to the stimuli were exactly the same. Her conscious was just along for the ride except she could think. Her body was just going through the motions. When she finally reached the finish point, she felt relieved and maybe a little bit proud of herself for how she got through it in real life. She had never really thought about after that night.

From there she is in the hospital watching the monitors going haywire and sending off alarms. Again fear filled her. She watched as the monitor for her baby dropped and hers went dangerously high then vice versa. She watched the lights as she was being rolled down the hall into the operating room. Remembering the doctor telling her not to bother counting, she wasn't going to be awake long enough. Then just like magic she disappeared again. This time she knew it was a drug-induced reason she disappeared.

"Dr. Guthrie, can I get your expertise on a patient?"

Dr. Sims began to explain how a patient that was transferred this morning was confusing him a bit. He explained how the patient had been in a car accident, airbags deployed, put her head through the windshield. For all medical purposes, she is unconscious, not responding to self or environment. However, the brain stem and the cerebral cortex are communicating. Her inability to respond can be an abnormality of consciousness and can include paralysis. It looks like a coma because she has zero responses and her eyes are rolled back and locked in place. Her EEG shows awake-like rhythms so no coma. Her locked-in state resembles catatonia but different. Her pain receptors are unresponsive. Her MRI shows no swelling, bleeding, or brain damage of any kind. If you look at her PET scan, it shows there is activity and a lot of it. The only area in grey is the area of the brain that registers pain. "What do you think?"

The two doctors go to where Delaney is laying. Dr. Guthrie takes a look at the monitors for a moment and asks about the bandage going around her head. He lifted her eyelids and shined his light across the white parts; her eyes were still rolled back. He poked her hand and foot with a needle, thumped a few muscles with no response.

"Hmm, I would take careful notes of this case because I see a write-up for the medical journals. The only explanation for it is more physiological and psychological than physical. If I had to take an educated guess, I would say there was some severe traumatic situation that she experienced which caused her to develop the ability to manipulate her mind and body to an extent of this magnitude, which is fascinating. I do not believe she is in a coma or a stage of catatonia. She is conscious but in some version of a locked-in state. Very interesting, her body seems to be resting while her brain is very active. I would keep her in ICU for observation. She seems to be controlling when she will awaken."

She seems to be controlling when she will awaken, that is what the voice said. Come on, Delaney, wake yourself up. Scream until they hear you. You have to wake up now. Something is not right. I have never not been able to wake myself up. I am screaming, but no sound is coming out, not even a moan. I can sense my body is not moving. Why? Why can't I wake up?

Reese and Ari arrived in Great Falls in no time. Ari called Jamison from the car when he realized he never called him back. They talked about how Jamison didn't think they would let Ari in to see her; he wasn't family or a spouse. Reese overheard him say that if he has to wait while Reese went in then so be it. He would just have to deal with whatever came.

Reese followed the signs to the ICU; there was a station where the nurse was very particular about who could go in and the rules of behavior. Both had to sign in. When she looked at the names, she raised an eyebrow towards Ari.

"What room is she in? Come on, Dad, I can't go in there without you."

Ari already had a blank stare on his face, so when his brain processed what Reese said they were already strolling down the hall towards her room. The rules were specific: no more than two, must remain calm, and must be on the quiet side.

"Why did you tell them I was your dad?"

"You heard the nurse; you wouldn't be allowed in otherwise, and like I said, I can't do this alone."

When they walked into the room, they could hear the monitors beeping. The other patient in there with her was on a ventilator that was moving up and down rhythmically. Her head was wrapped all the way around, her eyes were closed, wires were stuck to her head. She had an IV and about three monitors surrounding her bed. Reese pulled the chair out away from the wall and put it close to her bed. Tears started rolling down his cheeks as he began to whisper to her. Her face was really red and had cuts everywhere on it. She looked nothing like the woman who told him to the moon and back this morning. His mother laid there lifeless, and it made him afraid.

Mom, I can't do this without you. Please do not leave me. I need you. Fight, I know you are tired, but I need you to fight. She could hear him. Her heart was breaking. She started to pray to God to please help her wake up. She was out of ideas. No one noticed the tear that had physically fallen from her eye.

Dr. Sims came in to speak to both Reese and Ari. He started covering her injuries and the results of the tests they had been running since her arrival. He then went over to the computer and pulled up her PET scan; it was a rainbow of colors with a brain image as the background. The colors were changing slightly from frame to frame. Both Reese and Ari looked at the doctor in confusion and in desperate need of clarification.

"All these tests prove is there is no logical or medical reason that she should be in a locked-in state of mind or almost catatonic. She is conscious in some form but also unresponsive to any stimulation. All this activity being registered here is like a dream, a very vivid and in motion dream, that she is not ready to wake up from. It's like she is trapped in it and unwilling to be conscious in a medical definition. We believe it is more physiological than physical. We are going to keep her in the ICU overnight, but she really is not an intensive care patient. She is breathing on her own and has brain activity. She isn't in a coma, catatonic, or has any life-threatening injuries. The redness on her face is a chemical burn, allergic reaction to something from the airbag deployment. She didn't break any bones. She has minor abrasions and contusions, the contusion on her forehead being the worst. Her asthma gave them some difficulty since she went unconscious, and being hit with the airbags did not help. I am keeping her in ICU to monitor her and make sure she is out of the woods."

When the doctor was done, Reese asked where the restroom was. The doctor took him down the hall.

Ari sat in the chair, held her fingers, looking at the monitor on her finger.

"That doctor said you are in there and in some kind of conscious state, but you are in there. Maybe you are resting. Please wake up because I have so much to tell you. That young man you have raised and worked so hard at getting right is an outstanding human being, but he still needs you. I need you as well. I never realized what my life was missing until you came blowing in like a hurricane wind. I feel comfortable and complete when you are around, even when you challenge everything I think I am. I have been a better version of myself ever since you entered my life. Please don't leave now; I just found you. You have made me discover new things about myself that I never would have known without you. I need you to wake up so I can tell you what you mean to me. I have been trying to respect the fact that you are skittish when it comes to feelings. I am not going to spill my guts while you are not here to respond. Please come back to us."

Reese's phone rang, and he winced. His grandmother's name came up on caller ID. He knew better than to not answer it because she always call Mom's first. Reese took a deep breath and answered it hoping he would not give it away as to where he was and why.

"Nana, how is Hawaii?" A long pause while he listened because Nana could talk. She had no problem sucking the oxygen out of the room. "I believe she is out with Ari, but I know she has been having some trouble with her phone. First, it would answer itself, and sometimes it does not ring at all. She has been talking about getting a new one this weekend. She is still planning on picking you up at the airport." Then another long pause and Nana spoke. Reese was hiding in the bathroom so Nana could not hear the people or machines in the background. "Ok, Nana, I love you too and can't wait until you get home. If I see Mom soon I will let her know. Love you both too."

———✦———

"Come on, Mom, you got to wake up. I can't do that again. You don't want Nana to be mad at me."

Reese heard her voice way before he saw her.

"Aunt Mazy, we're down here once you sign in."

"OMG, she looks like that character from Harold and the other looking for burgers. She is going to hate that when she comes out of this. You know her stubborn ass is going to come out of this, probably with a couple new scars and another great story to tell. Any crazy bitch that has jumped out of helicopters and airplanes is not going to get taken out by a little bump on the head. Can she hear us?'

Ari stepped out to call Jamison and update him. Soon they were going to get kicked out of there for the night. There is a two-hour limit in the ICU.

Mazy leaned down and whispered in her ear, "Listen to me, Delaney Marie Delisle, you wake up right now and tell that man you love him. Don't you dare hide because you are afraid. You have never backed down from a challenge, so you suck it up, buttercup, and wake your ass up. I know you hear me. Not only does your son deserve to have many more years of your love but so does that man. He is looking very worried. I know you very well, and this is not like you at all. You look like shit, and I want you to wake up and argue with me. Soon their visiting hours end, and we will all be sent on our ways while you lay here. I can't even tell you how I think this sucks. Fight like hell to come back; never give up. You always say you are beautiful, you are strong, you are truly a badass bitch. You tell yourself that over and over again, and you make it happen."

Nine hours in. I am on my knees in front of my grandmother's headstone. Grandma, I can't express how much I miss you. I wish you were here right now to tell me how to get myself out of this. I am out of ideas, and you always had great advice. I sure could use some of that right now. I wish when you were alive I would have paid more attention to all the lessons you taught me. Just then she could feel her grandmother raking her fingernails along her scalp. "Oh, child, I am never too far. I watch." Yeah, but I rarely hear you speak to me. "Look at what you have seen since being in this deep. Basic training and the exercise you feared and thought you couldn't make it through. What did I tell you? I am strong, I am beautiful, I am a badass (smiling).

You thought you might die; it scared you. In the hospital, again you thought you were going to die; there, your thoughts were not as clear because they drugged you, but you were in there. See a pattern forming? Yes, I am here mostly because of my fear, which is how I learned to crawl deep into myself in the first place. So let's recap what you have seen so far: basic training where you conquered your fear and survived. Child-birth and motherhood where you didn't die and you are doing a pretty damn good job at motherhood, again conquering your fear. I am so proud of the woman you have be-come. So what fear has you here with me?"

I have been doing a lot of soul searching. You know that thing I like to tell people I don't have so they don't try to get close to me? I could hear my Grandmother laugh-ing. Well, I came to the conclusion that I love him, but I am so afraid of telling him. I think the accident was an opportunity that opened the door for me to crawl in and hide; now I can't figure out how to get myself out. Even though she never saw her grandmother she knew whole-heartedly she was there with her.

"Oh my child, in life there will be love, pain, fear, desires, and dreams. That is what waking up every day is all about, living life to the fullest and best of our ca-pabilities. Yes, when you love there is always the possibility of being hurt, a pain that can sometimes feel unbearable and make you think you never want to do it again. If you focus on that then you may never love again; that would be a shame, and you would rob yourself of one of life's greatest gifts. Love fills voids you didn't even know existed and supports you during the darkest hours. Your grandfather never stopped loving me even after I died. You have never stopped loving me nor I you, even though I am not physically there with you. To most people I am just a memory. Love makes me more than just a memory in your heart and mind. So tell me, why do you fear loving this man?"

He was married before, and it did not go as planned. It got bitter, horrible words and actions exchanged that left deep gashes, and he said it made his heart cold and numb. What if he is no longer capable of love, because of trust issues or lack of desire to invest in someone like that again? What if he never lets his heart be accessible to anyone no matter if trust issues disappear completely or not, keeping it prisoner. Plus that whole love thing still sometimes gives me the heebies. What if I don't love right? What if my past wrecks my future? What if I think I love him but really don't or worse? What if I love him and it's not enough, if I'm not enough?

"Now I understand your fear. Listen to me good; you know what happens when you assume. I do not need to beat you up with that. You already have ninja skills when it comes to beating up yourself and always have. Half of what you just said can be resolved by communicating with him and comprehending his response. He knows what you are, and when you're not afraid, your light shines bright and warms everything that chooses to bask in it. Let it shine so bright it drowns the darkness. Look at me as an example; your grandfather was not a fan of love when we met. Then I must have got under his skin, and we had a love that lasted past death. Sometimes things don't work out the way we want them to. When they don't it means your destiny has something different in store. Life has a way of changing: health, children, careers, people themselves, and even death. You are enough. If not for him, you are enough. You didn't do everything in your power to turn out to be a loving and caring woman to not be enough. You fought like hell, stumbling along the way, to survive and overcome. After being told your whole life your chance of having children was impossible, you feared when you found out you were pregnant. That was nothing compared to the fear you had during childbirth when you and he almost died. Look at your blessings; that boy tickles my funny bone and touches my heart. You love the right way for you. When you love, it has the force of hurricane winds that is you. Don't let your fear cripple you.

Eleventh hour: "Let's get another PET scan; the EEG is off the charts. I wish I knew where you are and what is happening. Your brain activity is fascinating. I do hope you remember this when you come back. I am very curious and I have questions." He shined the light in her eyes, but they were still rolled back and her body was still unresponsive. Her brain was looking like a dream, but her body was more like deep sleep, which typically slows everything down. Her breathing and pulse barely moved, but her brain activity very active. Her PET scan came back very colorful. Her brain was very active; both right and left hemisphere *were* incredibly engaged, resembled a moving rainbow.

Yes I do love hard, and that brings me to this fear; am I feeling love for him, or am I feeling something he is projecting? Or could it be all B.S. and I am just wishful thinking. I am almost positive it is me loving him and I am afraid to be vulnerable or hurt. *What if it is just the familiar taste of poison and I am just thinking about drinking it because I am feeling a little lonely? My pickiness is legendary and earned me a "man-eater" nickname, which I don't find flattering but kind of accurate.*

"Oh honey, in life there is love, pain, hope, faith, and fear. You may stumble, you may fall, but if you do not try you may never experience just how wonderful life may be. Your fear will keep you a prisoner until you stop any attempts at parole and just give up. No ma'am, I will haunt you and push you. I will not let you give up. You deserve to be loved, which probably would be easier to happen if you would just drop those fortress walls of yours and unlock some of those padlocks you keep that heart of yours imprisoned in."

I hear you, Grandma, which leads me to my more pressing problem. I am here, not really sure how I got here. I don't think I have ever been this deep before. I have tried screaming, slapping myself, everything I could think of to wake up. I don't know what to do to get back out.

"Honey, I don't know how to help you. You used to worry me with the way your mind worked. I wasn't the only one. I remember those doctors gathered around you discussing you with all those wires hooked to your head while you slept, whatever that test was when they ruled out you having epilepsy to try to explain your visions. Heaven help you if they ever figured out there was more, a lot more. They already acted like scientists trying to dissect the specimen, practically drooling on themselves. Gives me the chills just thinking about it."

You made me promise to never tell you if I had visions about you; that was the hardest promise I ever made in my life. I fought it with everything in me when it happened, but I couldn't and wouldn't break my promise. Why did you make me promise?

"My faith in God. I think he gave you the visions to help everyone, but as far as I was concerned, it was what God had in store for me. Besides, you cannot alter the outcome and never have been able to. The bad still happens: car crashes, blood clots, heart attacks, and so many more that you can't change or stop. You see what you see; you feel more than most. You already have to hide it because close-minded people will never understand it. I remember how pissed you were when you got called a witch and a freak. You have a gift, even when it doesn't feel like that. You are a fire that burns bright and hot; some will get burned by the truth that reveals itself to you while others *bask in the warmth. If this man hasn't insulted you or ran, he doesn't fear the truth or you. Lord knows you have taken this man on a journey he has never seen the likes of and he hasn't backed down. I pray you have found the one that can handle you, all of you to include everything you hide even though you never pretend to be something you are not. You are very guilty of not letting people see the entire version of you, which I completely understand because most can't handle it. Have some faith my dear."*

And just like that, she was gone in a void of existence. Last thought was how long had she been there. Will she ever come back to the real world? She could hear the silence start to creep in and the darkness start to close in until I can see anything. I only hear whispers for a short period longer. I feel heavy, and everything starts to fade. I really wonder where I go.

Twelfth hour: Ari and Reese arrived at the hospital as soon as they would let them. Both sat in silence listening to the machines and monitors in the room while each said a prayer and were lost in their thoughts. The doctor already told them he was hoping she would wake up before they moved her to a room on a lower floor. She showed no signs of life threatening injuries and did not need intensive care.

Delaney came walking up to her dining room table and ran her fingers along the smoothness. It did not feel like it usually does. Then she saw the bouquet of roses Ari got her. They were even more beautiful than she remembered them: full bloom and the colors popped. Then she saw the woman standing at the other end of the table. Her smile was warm and inviting. Something about her was familiar but also not at the same time. The woman stood there watching her for a moment until Delaney spoke. Do I know you?

"In a sense, but that is not a matter for this moment. You do not belong here and you must go back." She thought of Reese and looked at the flowers. "Ari is pacing inside himself because he lost someone else he loved very much in this room many years ago, while trying to portray being strong for your Reese. He is praying for help. That young man is praying to God to please not take his mother. You are his world. That doesn't last forever, and you do not want to waste a single moment of it. You hold their hands when they are little then you look and they are grown men holding your hand." She looked away for a second. "He is not ready to be on his own, and he is not ready to be without you; neither of them are. You have not left that man's mind since the siren

went by his house—actually way before then. I fear for him and your son if you do not go back soon. Your son is on the brink of adulthood, and that is something to be cherished. You see the adult they become and how they function and navigate their way through life, love, and everything in-between. You do not want to miss a single moment of that, which means it's time for you to go back. Besides, you know why you came here, and you have no doubts about how you feel. It is time to confess how you feel to him, and you can't do that here in this place. Your light is not meant to be hidden in here. Taking your light away from those who find strength and comfort from it will cause part of themselves to die. I know you would never intentionally yield that knife."

I wish I knew how to get back. I tried screaming, jumping into my body like I was out of it, tried picturing myself waking up, all kinds of things. None of it has worked for me yet. I keep the whispers from those outside of this place but cannot reply to them; they don't hear me. I have never been this far in before, and I am definitely feeling lost. I want nothing more than to get back to the ones I love.

"Funny how you mention love, you kind of stressed yourself a bit over that word. Did you know he was there? After your crash? You must have because you tried to tell him it as if you knew he was there. Then your stress level took over on top of your asthma and injuries, leading us to here. You let the fear bring you here; granted like you said deeper than you used to go, but it was how you coped. Each conversation and event coping with that fear one step at a time. So, Delaney, if fear brings you here, what takes you back to where you want to be?"

Delaney ran her hand over the roses and thought of Reese closing her eyes. She opened them, gasping as the woman backed away fading.

"Irene, wait," reaching her hand out.

Ari jumped out of the chair to his feet dropping Delaney's hand that hit the bed rail knocking a monitor off her finger. She opened her eyes slowly, unsure of where she was. By this time, Reese is calling for the doctor. The monitor had already alerted the nurse's station. Delaney said nothing just blinked while getting her bearings. Her memories of all of it crashing into her like she did the windshield. Reese was so happy, tears started to roll down his cheeks; then he crashed into her chest, thanking God, and just hugging her. She tried not to wince at the pain. The doctor came in and took her vitals and checked her eyes before he asked her questions about whether she knew where she was and what had happened. Her answers were short and delivered from a very dry and scratchy throat. Her chest had felt like she had been sacked by a defensive lineman. It hurt everywhere. She listened as the doctor spoke about her injuries and she was going to move to another room. If all went well she would be able to go home soon, not today though. He wanted her under observation for a bit to ensure she was alright. Ari is still looking like he has seen a ghost.

A few hours later, she is in her new room with some of the monitors and wires gone. Ari and Reese had gone down to the gift shop to find her a pair of sweats since being informed her clothes were covered in blood and glass shards. The nurse recommended she not wear them home for safety sakes. She must have dozed off before Jamison had come in. He sat and started talking. She didn't know how much she missed before she woke.

"Delaney, I am not good at this; I hate hospitals. I have been that way since we came and picked up Ari after his parents died in this very hospital. Part of him died that day, and he will lose another part of himself if you do not wake up and do that voodoo you to him he has grown so fond of."

"I am awake."

Jamison about flew out of the chair.

"That is twice today that I have made men jump. I am not that special, but y'all got me feeling pretty powerful."

"Holy shit, woman, what the hell is wrong with you? You trying to land me in here with a heart attack? Where are Ari and Reese?" She replied with a slight shrug and shake of her head. "I am amazed your watchdogs wandered off to be honest with you. If it weren't for the hospital forcing them out of here, they never would have left. They were at my place last night, up all night, eating everything in site while pacing my floors." She smiled at the thought that they at least didn't starve in her absence. "You really did scare the shit out of both of them. By the way, that kid of yours is pretty cool and has a good mind for engineering. He is going to go places. Ari on the other hand is wreck. Plus what you said as you woke confirmed there is a voodoo that you do like only you can," *chuckling*, "even got some doctors whispering about you being some strange case. I got to tell you I think they are right; you are a strange case, Delaney the Mail Lady. Oh yeah, my mail person is a pudgy middle age man; can you work on that for me?"

Ari and Reese came in carrying a bag from a local store and coffee cups. Better be a Dew hidden in that damn bag since they hooked themselves up.

"We had to get you something to wear that would fit. The gift shop didn't have sweat pants, only tops and not anything you would be happy wearing, until then you are stuck with that really attractive gown that your butt hangs out the back that matches that turban bandage you are rocking." All three of them chuckling, Jamison laughing about how only a teenage child can tell a woman she looks like shit and get away with it, ass hanging out and all. "Well, Mom, there is a nice cold beverage in that bag that I will never give you a hard time about drinking again; just don't get caught with it or I will insinuate Jamison brought it to you."

Delaney tried to stop laughing because of the pain in her chest and everywhere else. She could feel their eyes on her like hawks when she got out of the bed to use the restroom. She held her gown shut in the back making sure not to flash her ass in the granny panties the hospital found for her since hers were full of glass. This time she avoided looking into the mirror at her face; it was too much the first time. She was red and cut up from her head to her knees. Her inner thighs had bruises the size of softballs where she must have tensed and squeezed the shit out of her automatic on the floor. She can already tell she is going to have some new permanent scars from this little excursion. While she sits there looking at the damage, her thoughts drifted to the fact that she still needs to tell Ari how she feels and let the chips fall where they may.

I am one with my light side and my dark side, my past, and my gift. I know how hard I am to love because I am not normal in conventional thinking. I will never be anything but myself; however, most people will never truly know me because I will never let them see me. The gift helps me most of the time in that department. I will be forever haunted by the "what ifs" if I even thought about or tried to run now. I hear his safe word Courage whispered in my head. I will start to crumble on the inside if I do not confess to him how I feel soon. I can feel the winds spinning inside gathering the debris for mass destruction since I have my hurricane contained within.

Shortly after Dr. Sims came in to review my chart and let me know he wants me to do a couple tests later this afternoon, results pending me being able to go home tomorrow. A few hours later, the guys left to go eat and get cleaned up. About thirty minutes later, a nurse came and got me to take me down for another PET scan. Dr. Sims was waiting as we got me hooked up. Relax and stay as still as possible. I could close my eyes, and he warned me he was going to didn't see any problems with it. Monitors attached to my chest and my head, I figured it was easiest to close my eyes.

I could hear him record date, time, and basic female stats; then we began. At first there were no questions; then he explained for me to give my answers in as much detail as possible. That was when my spider senses started tingling hard. The first question was about my accident and what did I feel and remember. Easy. Then he asked when I lost consciousness, but he paused on that word. The word distracting popped into my head and made me smile. I told him it was as they took me out of the car and were getting ready to bring me here.

"Do you mean when you were being taken to your local hospital?"

Shit, I am in Great Falls not in Trave. I don't remember that part.

"Yes, when I was going in the ambulance. I could hear some stuff like my stats, and I remember epinephrine needle to chest and the burn of my inhaler, but I don't remember using it because I couldn't reach it."

He looked at her medical file and recorded how I was unconscious at the time of epinephrine administration and nebulizer with asthma medication.

"Delaney, where did you go during that time?"

"I don't understand the question."

"Did you go somewhere, a location, a dream? How did you get there, and what was happening?"

Crap, crap, he is fishing for something. Think before you answer this; you will not look good in a sleeveless jacket being poked and prodded constantly. Besides, he can't prove anything.

"I was dreaming; it was all kind of random not making much sense. I felt like I could hear things going on around me sometimes, but it was like whispers in a dream. None of it would have been of significance except to me." *Which is true.* "As for how I get there, I have no idea." *Also not a complete lie; yes I sort of know how I crawl into myself, and it all stems from trauma in my past and creating that for survival. As for being in there and not being able to come out, I have no idea how that happened.*

There were a few more questions, but it feels like he is a little disappointed in not getting the answers he was hoping for. I did a lot of not understanding the question until I had a not bat-shit crazy answer for it without revealing too much about how that talent came about. Plus, the scenes were for my personal use in dealing with the stress about realizing that I do truly love Ari and how I need to tell him. After the test, I was wheeled back to my room and was kind of quiet about the whole thing when the guys returned smelling better.

Time to go home.

CHAPTER 11

She was having a tough time getting around a bit. Soreness was still a factor. She was not allowed to go back to work for 72 hours. She figured she would use one of those days to get the van ready to run the route. That was not her favorite to drive for that many hours per day. The plastic console hurts her ass by the end of the day. She still gets tired a lot and decided to curl up on the couch and rest for a bit. One of her babysitters were there to keep a watchful eye on her like they have been since her accident. Tomorrow part of her time will be occupied going to the airport to pick her parents up; she is already dreading explaining what she will be doing. Plus it was still eating at her insides how to tell Ari that she loved him.

She just closed her eyes for a moment. Then she was sleeping hard. She was not sure how long she had been out. Time had still been eluding her a bit since the accident. The sands of time shattered. There was a note from Ari at the coffee table for her. *Had to run to my house for just a moment to take care of some business and grab a few things. I could not bring myself to wake you. Hopefully, I will be back and you will still be resting.* She needed a shower and clean clothes but she was dreading the shower. The water stung her face and cuts. Her mind needed the peace of a nice relaxing shower once she got past the pain.

She turned the hot water on and held her breath as she stepped into the water. It stung like hell for a minute. The pain got her mind spinning in multiple directions. She could have died in that wreck; things could have gone so differently. The woman at her table was right; there was a familiarity about her, but she was right it was not her time yet. She started thinking about how she was not going to take this blessing for granted. Her heart broke at the thought of leaving her son. Then Ari dominated her brain. She started to realize she needed to tell him how she felt. While she was within herself she could sense her need to confess and soon. Was she terrified to tell him? Oh hell yes. Mr. Distracted was a huge distraction to her. She loved him and that terrified her, not nearly as much as telling him. The more she thought about it the more it ate at her insides. She felt so overwhelmed and frustrated that she leaned her head into the wall and let go. Tears flowed down; those tears then turned to sobs. Quiet but relentless sobs.

Ari arrived back to Delaney's feeling real good about himself and all he got accomplished. He felt as if he did the right thing. He was not sure how she was going to react, and he was a little worried about that. When he walked into the living room, he saw she was no longer sleeping on the couch; she also was nowhere to be seen. He wandered through the house looking for her. He could hear the shower running, but he could also hear something else. He put his ear to the door and listened for a moment. What he heard pulled at his heartstrings; as much as he thought about her privacy was also as much as he thought about her being in pain or worse.

He slowly opened the door and peaked in. "Delaney, are you alright?"

"Yes. No. I don't know. I really don't know." *A long pause and he was not sure what he should do.* "My thoughts are spiraling around in my head. I want to say something, and have been trying to for a while now, but I do not know how to." *Then she leaned her forehead back into the wall while the water hit the back of her shoulders.* "I don't know. I don't even know what I am trying to say."

Ari took off his shoes and jacket and stepped into the shower with the rest of his clothes on. He walked up behind her, putting his hands on her shoulders to spin her around. "Talk to me. Are you hurt? What can I do for you?"

The tears began to stream down her face, her knees felt weak, and she was even holding her breath. She had to grab life by the reins and stop this torment she was feeling inside. It was time to tell him how she felt, and she was trying to figure out the words to say. Right now the words and feelings swirling around were not organized or coherent, and she felt as if it would come out sounding like a foreign language. She didn't speak for a moment.

"Delaney, you have had something on your mind for a while now." He put both hands on her face and made her look at him. "You have been quiet and keeping to yourself on the inside, and that is the part of your life I want to know as well. I can handle more than you give me credit for. I can handle the good, bad, ugly, and I believe I can even handle the hurricane you can be. The voodoo you do doesn't even scare me. The only thought that is scaring me right now is you pulling away from me and a fear that you are going to run or you are hurt more from that accident than you are letting on. Please talk to me, honey; tell me what is troubling you."

She stared at him for a moment in disbelief; running was the last thing from her mind— well maybe, but at the same time running straight into his arms. Her head was a scrambled mess. Here she is standing completely naked, stripped of any kind of protection but her mind, which puts her in direct battle with her heart, vulnerable from every direction. Time felt like it was standing still and he was standing ready, waiting.

She took a deep breath and swallowed hard. "I am not thinking about running. For the first time in a long time I am not thinking about running in any manner. What I have been trying to hide and not being completely successful at has nothing to do with running. I have been quiet because I have been trying to sort things out in my head. You made me believe, you made me hope, you have broken through my defenses one by one until you are so close I sense your very being in my soul. My heart was shut off for self-preservation reasons. Now it feels like my world came crashing in on me. I have been so guarded for so long that when this happened I didn't know what to do. I felt lost. It's not that I am a cold-hearted bitch, but I wasn't about to hand my heart over to someone who didn't understand it or would not respect it. Before I could detect or stop what was happening to me because I do not always trust my heart being an empath, not sure if it is their feelings I feel or my own, I feel as if it can betray me in secret. For as strong as I am, I am also just as sensitive and weak—resilient and a fighter. Somewhere along our journey, a storm started raging within the confines of me. I was standing in the eye of that hurricane after my accident until I was positively sure I could get past my fear of *my* feelings. I was scared because I did not know how to get back once I realized I was ready to confess my behavior."

"Delaney, do you love me?"

"Ari, yes I love you. I know how hard I am to love because I am so weird. With that being said, I love with the gale force winds of a hurricane, debris and all. You might need your running shoes instead of me."

He leaned his forehead into hers. "Listen to me, Delaney Delisle; I am not going to run. You make me see stars when the skies are dark. Since the day you blew through my door I have been yours. Your winds wrapped around me pulling me to you, filled my lungs with your warmth and life force. Sometimes it was a little messy...a little adventurous and kinky...and makes every part of me spark with an excitement for each new day. You are not hard to love. I know because I have loved you for a while now. In the hospital, when you called out to Irene as you woke, it sealed my fate. I am yours, and you are mine, now and always. Make no mistake in your gift. I love you more and more with each moment."

He shut the water off, grabbed the bath sheet, and wrapped it around her body gently. Stripped his soaked clothes and left them on the shower floor. Then he swooped her up in his arms and carried her off to the bedroom. He gently set her on the bed and crawled up behind her, holding her tight to make sure he was not dreaming. She slept in his arms. The closeness and electricity was calming both their storms.

After the most intimate session of love making, it was time to head to the airport. Her mother gave her grief, and Ari could hear the fear in her voice as she looked at the cuts and bruises Delaney was covered in. It was a rough ride to home to watch Delaney be put in such an uncomfortable situation. He knew if she could run at that very moment she would be gone. On top of that, she was talking with her dad about getting the van ready to run her route in two days while they pushed her to get the right-hand Jeep she had been looking at. She already had checked on getting the car fixed, but the airbag replacements cost more than the car was worth.

They had just started to unload bags from the car when the tow truck showed up with her car. They walked the truck to an open area between the two houses. Her mother watched intently as the car came off the flatbed with the realization of it all. The windshield had a forehead mark that tore it open and shattered it to tiny pieces. The airbags were still dangling from the dash covered in brown stains of dried blood. There was a two-foot long chunk of hair blowing in the wind off the tear in the windshield. Front of the car was only slightly banged up. Most of the damage happened inside of the car. There were glass shards and cubes on both seats and the floor. Her mother stared at the car turning multiple shades of white. Ari said a prayer as he looked on, thanking God for not taking her, for letting her be standing here, alive.

"Thank God you got a thick ass skull," Nana said as she stared at the windshield while Delaney looked at car in horror of every scary moment while in there and after flooded her brain. The in-between time of her being there and somewhere else at the same time.

Delaney, not wanting to think about it anymore, went back to the car to finish unloading her parents' luggage. Mom looked at the car a while longer not saying a word. Dad just shook his head and said how lucky she was. Ari went and helped Delaney finish unloading before they headed back to her place.

On the way back to her place, she stopped at the car and popped open the door. She began looking for something with an intensity and urgency. "Babe, what are you looking for?"

"My cross, the one my grandmother gave me. I need to find it; it has to be with me."

They looked from the front end of that car to the back. It was starting to get dark, and the broken glass left little cuts where you rubbed your hands across it without knowing it was there. They found the review mirror or what was left of it under the driver's seat. The shattered pieces of that car were a grim reminder that it could have been a lot worse and by the looks of it should have been.

"It's getting dark; we will look for it again in the morning. We will find it. I know it is important to you."

On the way back to the house, Ari took out his wallet and pulled a picture from the pocket.

"Do you recognize them?"

"I don't recognize him but her I do. She was the woman at my dining table talking to me. Telling me things. Why?" *Trying to be real careful how she worded things to him.*

"That is my mother Irene and my father. Irene is the name you yelled out when you woke up reaching; that is why I leaped from the chair. You called out for my mother."

"Oh." Then she replayed the conversation. His mother was the woman he lost in that very same room at that very same hospital. His mother came to me to tell me how I needed to get back, back to her son and mine. She was there to guide me home. All of a sudden her familiar feeling made complete sense. "Ooohhh!"

After arriving back at the house, she was feeling mentally drained and knew that the van was waiting for her. They decided on delivery and the van could wait until morning. It wasn't going anywhere and should not take much to be road ready. It had only been in the garage for a few months. Ari even volunteered to help although his skills were not as vast as hers.

CHAPTER 12

*I*n the morning, Delaney and her dad were in the garage getting the van prepared to hit her route running. Fluids were being topped off, tires checked, and ensuring everything was as capable and ready as possible. Because her garage is cordwood as well as her house, she did not hear the vehicle pull up outside. She had no idea what was transpiring right underneath her nose; she had a bit of tunnel vision going on.

Delaney's mother had come into the garage side entrance and ordered them to take a momentary break and come outside to explain to her what the hell is going on. Delaney looked at her dad for guidance, and he just shrugged. Slowly she got out of the van and followed her mom and dad out of the garage. Once she got across the cement pad, she noticed it on her left.

Ari was standing there holding the right side door open on a white Jeep next to her garage. She froze in place for a second, not real sure how to move, or if she could. Then her mom pushed her from behind in the direction she was supposed to go. All she could do was stare at Ari in disbelief. It was the Jeep, the right-hand Jeep she had been contemplating purchasing. *What was it doing here? Why is it here?* She kept moving until she was right in front of him; he waved his hand motioning her to get into it. She did as instructed and got into the vehicle. It felt so different and foreign, but so comfortable.

"Do you like it? Can you picture yourself delivering out of it?"

"I can, but how did you do this and when? Why?"

Reese started laughing and telling Ari he owed him ten bucks, easiest money he ever made. That was when Delaney got a real confused look on her face, figuring there was some inside joke she was not privy to at the time. She ran her hand along the steering wheel and looked in the back at the space. Then she noticed the left seat was gone and a rack was put in its place. It was set up for success.

"I even found your cross." Instinctively she reached up and grabbed ahold of it without looking; then she froze. It felt different, very different. "I know the chain is a little shorter, but we will remedy that." That was not what made it feel different, and he knew it. It took a moment for her brain to kick in and register what her hand was feeling. What she felt poked her fingertip. She looked at Ari leaning into the open window sill; then she looked at her hand holding the cross, then back to Ari. The grin on his face said it all. She looked back at her hand and spun the cross around. Right there, on the back, was a gold ring that shined in the sunlight.

Ari cleared his throat. "Delaney Marie DeLisle, will you marry me and be the only one to handle *all* my packages from here on out and forever?"

Nana has tears streaming down her cheeks. Reese is looking on with an intensity of anticipation. Dad is just holding his breath because he knows his little girl and he knows you never can tell what is going to come out of that mouth of hers. As far as he is concerned, it's a 50/50 shot here, could go either way.

She blinked a few times in shock, giggled, and turned to face him and give him his answer.

EPILOGUE

Reese and Abby arrive fashionably late as usual. As Ari walks toward them to steal his second favorite little ball of energy, Reese informed him to stop where he was. He bent down and let Ana get her footing then he let go of her. She let out a shrill "Bepa" giggling and cooing as she stomped across the tiles in her little shoes. She was stomping her way right over to her Bepa. Before I could stop it, Charlie came running out of nowhere, nails clicking across the same tiles and plowed right into her, licking her face once he had her down. That just made her giggle more. "Charlie! Bepa, you better save your Anabelle before Charlie claims her as his." Ari reached down and picked her up hugging her and pretending he was going to drop her. Charlie was dancing around his feet ready to catch the little pistol pot.

"Look at you, Grandpa, but it actually suits you. Hard to believe it's been 10 years since you stole government property and claimed it to be yours and yours alone. Tainting your friends with your adventures and kink escapades along the way. Tsk, tsk, my brother. Who's that big girl stealing hearts everywhere?" *Making Ana squeeze Ari tight and smile at Jamison*

"One day I hope you have all of this and more. You got a good start with that wife of yours. You wear that happiness well, brother." *Both watching as their wives chat about photos on the mantle.*

"Look at us, all domesticated and shit. Well, I have to admit 10 years ago I never would have pictured us here. Married and married with families. I'm not complaining by no means. You almost lost her, and she did that voodoo she does so well and introduced me to the love of my life I never knew I wanted until it happened."

The ladies moved to the kitchen to grab the dinner stuff and start hauling it to the living room. It was when Gabrielle stopped at the kitchen sink for a drink of water.

"You haven't told him yet. When you do, do not take his initial reaction at face value; it will be shock."

Gabrielle turned around to face Delaney with a questioning look on her face. Abby looked up from grabbing silverware to look at the other two ladies and stood still.

"What are you talking about?"

"If I had to guess, she is talking about... *pregnancy*," *in a whisper.* "You will get used to her doing that; she doesn't control it well. What? I have been there; you are the whole reason I went to the doctor and found out for sure. Don't try to figure out how she knows things like that; you will drive yourself crazy. Just roll with it."

"How do you... I just found out, and I am not real sure how to tell him yet."

"You'll know when the time is right, just don't look at his initial reaction as anything other than the shock it will be. After he chats with Ari, all will be exactly as it is meant to be. He will be a good and loving dad with your help of course."

The ladies take the rest of dinner to the table and gather around for toasts and the ten years of stories that keep their lives interesting. Delaney rubs the scars on her forehead and looks to see the life and love that surrounds her. New adventures await, new life coming, and she had to say thank you to God for letting her be here to be a part of it all.

CPSIA information can be obtained
at www.ICGtesting.com
Printed in the USA
BVHW042057261121
622645BV00012B/700